VAMPIRE SEEKER

THE SAMANTHA CARTER SERIES

TIM O'ROURKE

VAMPIRE SEEKER

THE SAMANTHA CARTER SERIES

piatkus

PIATKUS

First published in Great Britain in 2014 by Piatkus

A CIP catalogue record for this book
is available from the British Library.

ISBN 978-0-349-40210-9

Typeset in Sabon by Palimpsest Book Production Ltd, Falkirk, Stirlingshire
Printed and bound in Great Britain by Clays Ltd, St Ives plc

Papers used by Piatkus are from well-managed forests
and other responsible sources.

MIX
Paper from
responsible sources
FSC® C104740

Piatkus
An imprint of
Little, Brown Book Group
100 Victoria Embankment
London EC4Y 0DY

An Hachette UK Company
www.hachette.co.uk

www.piatkus.co.uk

For Lynda – My Cowgirl!

ACKNOWLEDGEMENTS

After more rejection letters than I could afford the stamps for, I decided to self-publish my books in March 2011. At first things were slow but I persisted. Come September the same year my self-published books started to sell and by October 2011 I had sold over 10,000 copies of my books. This was more than I could have ever imagined in my wildest dreams and I wondered when the bubble word burst. As yet it hasn't and my self-published books continued to sell. By September 2013 I will have sold in excess of a quarter of a million of my self-published books.

I publish my books from my kitchen in Buckinghamshire, England. Pretty much everything is done here. But it has taken more than just me, an overactive imagination and my laptop to make my books a success. There are plenty of people I need to thank along the way. Firstly, my beautiful wife, Lynda, who is brutal in her assessment of my work. She worries little about telling me where I'm going wrong – she is my harshest critic. I'd like to thank my three sons, Joseph, Thomas and Zachary for tiptoeing through the kitchen while I'm lost in my world of writing and Valarie and David Cooper for their support and encouragement. A really special thank you to Patrick Taylor who gave me my first ever typewriter all the way back in 1985 and would sit with me for hours and correct my terrible spelling and grammar. Cris Ramis, Marc Ramis and Linda Ramis for being my second family and who used to read the stories I wrote when I was an acne-ridden 15-year-old! You guys helped me through a lot. Thank you. I owe a massive debt of thanks to Carles Barrios, for creating me the best of covers for my books and for being such a great guy to work with (hugs!). Big thank you to Carolyn Johnson Pinard for weeding out the mistakes! Thanks to Holly Harper for starting the Facebook fan club, you're a star. I'd like to thank Ed Fenton who was the first person outside of my family to read my work and gave me the confidence to believe in my writing – that meant more to me than you'll ever know. I would also like to thank my agent Peter Buckman who took a chance on me and my vampires and werewolves. Thanks also to Harry Bingham for your support and honest feedback. And a special thank you to Anna Boatman for believing in me.

There are so many people I would like and probably

need to thank, but none so much as those loyal fans who have tirelessly supported me and my books. Without you guys none of this would have ever happened and I can't thank you enough. I love chatting to you all on Facebook and various other sites on the internet. So I would just like to say a big thank you to the following fans and book bloggers for your encouragement and unwavering support:

Lisa Ammari, Carles Barrios, Sharra Courter Turner, Louise Pearson, Louise Chapman, Caroline Barker, Shana Benedict, Jen Rosenkrans Montgomery, Gayle Morell, Louise Kemp, Sally Cannell, Kerry Goddard, Holly Harper, Robbie Parker, Daisy Kennedy, Nicole Leonard, Arista McKim, Craig McKim, Jennifer Goehl, Jennifer Martin Green, Nereid Gwilliams, Claire White, Michelle Wilton, Kiera Spencer-Hayles, Kerry Anne Porter, Jane Barron, Ally Esmonde, Craig Phillips, Ben Munro, Cally Munn, Helen Websdale, Noreen McCartan-Doran, Lekeisha Thomas, Sonya Avramoska, DiAnn Fields, Paul Goddard, Steve Boston, Lisa Darke, Gerrard Collins, Lois Li, Karen Neill, Richard Ayres, Bree Pearsall, Aminah Ahmad, Sue McGarvie, Charlene Attard, Bernice Thomas, Stacy Szita, Ronda Lynch, Stephanie Beckett, Maria Vargas, Jacqui Platts, Claire Graham, Mark Gallard, Michelle Harlow, Becky Fisk, Deanna Schultz, Andrew Patterson, Amanda Patterson, Janice.A.Scott, Emma Rapley, Warren Bixby, Heather

Braunberger Barela, Emma Graves, Paul Collins, Connie Neville, Shawnette Hocson, Kay Donley, Jill Andrew, Peggy Ryan, Jennifer Bryson, Becky Lees, Teresa Walsh, Beth Husselbee-Orwin, Hazel Pattison, Monique Bouvier Grasso, Sarah Curry, Rebecca Holloway, Sarah Parker, Jaala Larsen, Amber Mundwiller, Sharon Ward, Toni Francis, Sheila Urbanski, Amanda Porter, Nichola Dickson, Judi Hargraves, Kayleigh Griffiths, Savannah Gavin Harrop, Beata Janik, Louise At Readers Confession, Nikki Shreim, Tara Taggart, Micky Blue Skies Stewart, Lisa Rachelle Wolper, Kerrie Watling, Kim Odaniel, Hannah Landsburgh, Tammie Silva, Patrycja Nowacka, Stacey Hoy, Courtney Jackson, Rosie Dargue, Conny HK, Mandy Foster Meier, Tanya Bobrucki, Jackie McLeish, Wendy Wiegert, Barbara Grubb, Rose Lennart, Sarah Lane, Julie Garner Shaw, Dollie Lemon, Eric Townsend, Abbie Robertson, Rachel Roddy, Claire Ashmore, Diane Hurditch, Carolyn Johnson Pinard, Autumn Nauling, Silvia Roman Villanueva, Cherry Crawford, Erica Paddock, Jemma Wood, Shelly McKelvey, Cassie Sansom, Jenn Waterman, Patricia Lavery, Alison Phillips, Jamie Harris, Penny McCoy, Lindy Roberts, Fiz Halliwell, Claire O'neil, Sam Mcmullen, Lianne Lewis-Devillie, Stacey Tucker, Shelly Horner, Dianna Butler, Lisa Kresco-Churchey, Angela Hubbs, Heidi Madgwick, Shelby Proudfoot, Fiona Nelson, Rebecca Smith, Phoenix 2000, Jessica Johnson.

A big thank you to the following book bloggers/ reviewers:

Shana at bookvacations.wordpress.com
Darkfallen & Greta at Paranormalwastelands.blogspot. com
Braine & Cimmaron at Talkingsupe.com
Nikki Archer at vampsandstuff.com
Bella at paranormal book club
Caroline Barker at Areadersreviewblog.wordpress.com
Jessica Johnson Bookend2Bookend
Phoenix2000

I mentioned right at the beginning of this note of thanks that I *persisted* – and that's the whole point. Don't ever let anyone tell you you *can't*. You *can* if you really want to!

Take care,
Tim O'Rourke

PART ONE

The Preacher

1

My name is Samantha Carter, Sammy for short, and the man I'm following stepped like a shadow from the alleyway and out into the drizzle. He glanced back only once and pulled the collar of his knee-length coat up about his throat. I pressed myself flat against the wall and gripped the bottle of holy water which I held in my hand. The other held the police scanner, and I placed it against my ear.

"We have another one," a voice crackled.

"What is your location?" another voice hissed, as if coming from another time.

"Braham Street, at the back of Sedgwick Court," the voice wavered. "Oh, Jesus, he's taken the head this time. The body doesn't have a head."

I stepped out of the shadows and watched the figure

hurry up Mansell Street. There was very little traffic. The only sound was the shrill *whoop-whoop* of sirens approaching from the distance, and the blue and white glare of flashing emergency lights from behind Sedgwick Court, where the killer's latest victim lay strewn across a square patch of grass in the dark and falling rain.

I watched the man head in the direction of Aldgate High Street and followed. I'd had a pretty shitty week to be honest, and something told me things were only going to get worse. Karl, who I had been seeing for the last six months, finally got so mad at me that he left my flat, slamming the door behind him, and I hadn't heard from him since. Not even a text. The sex had been good, not mind-blowing, but he had been kind and had made me laugh with his goofy ways. Was I upset? Not much. I had other things on my mind – like the man I was now following.

Anyhow, I'm only twenty-two, and who needs to be bogged down with someone else's demands? Not that Karl was ever really demanding, but he did get pissed off with me, as I always had a cigarette dangling from the corner of my mouth, my head in a book, or I was searching the Internet, trying to prove that *they* really do exist. I'm not a cop or anything like that – no such excitement for me. But I do study criminology at the City University in London. My other *thing* is the study of vampires. Now, as far as I know there isn't any university in the world where you can study such things

– shame really, as I know it would be my dream. Karl would say in a jokey kind of way that I'd only take my head out of the books if he were as white as a bar of soap, had fangs, and a set of claws.

But Karl just didn't get it – not really. I didn't want to shag one of these creatures – I just wanted to capture one. I wanted to capture the one who had killed four women in the last three months across London. The press said that 'Jack was back', as they believed that the murders were being carried out by a Jack the Ripper copycat. But that was just crap. Sure, the murders had been brutal. Each of the women had been mutilated; their throats slashed open to the point of decapitation, and then all had been stabbed several times in the abdomen. A lot of similarities, but that's where they ended. The original murders had taken place in 1888, when there was little or no forensic science. Offender profiling was a science yet to be dreamt up. But today was different – very few serial killers got away with their hideous crimes. He left no clues. In a city with over sixty thousand CCTV cameras, the killer hadn't been captured on one of them. Not even a glimpse, or a shadow. It was like he had just disappeared. There were other differences, too.

Apart from the fact that the murders had taken place on different dates and locations than the original killings, the wounds inflicted on the victims hadn't been made by knives, and there was no blood discovered at the scenes of the crimes. How did I know this? Sally, who I shared my flat with, had been dating an officer from the Metropolitan Police Force. He was a search officer who had been placed on the inner cordon after the second killing. During a drunken night of shagging, he had let slip to her that the forensic teams at the scene had been puzzled by the fact that the victim had been completely drained of blood. It was as if whoever had carried out the frenzied attack had licked up every last drop of blood. He also confided in Sally that the wounds looked as if they had been made by a set of claws, instead of a knife or other sharply pointed instrument. Why he felt the need to tell my friend this while they were shagging, I will never know. But Sally was writing her first-year paper on forensically aware killers, and she was real pretty – and she probably seduced the information out of him.

Armed with this knowledge, I knew the murders were the work of a vampire. I know – crazy idea, right? But why? Is it any dafter than those who spend their lives trying to prove the existence of aliens, Bigfoot, the Loch Ness Monster, pixies, fairies – or whatever else turns people like me on? What I mean is, vampires don't turn me on – but the thought of proving they exist, does. What lengths would I go to to get proof? Standing in a dark alleyway, late at night, with a pocketful of garlic, a bottle of holy water in my hand, a crucifix around my neck, and a police scanner pressed to my ear – that's how far I would go.

A helicopter buzzed overhead, a single beam of light shining from its belly, lighting up the streets below, frantically trying to locate the killer.

"To all units," the police scanner crackled in my ear again, "the suspect must still be in the immediate vicinity."

"Do we have a description?" another officer asked.

"Not at this time," the original voice came back, sounding frustrated.

The man in the long dark coat reached the top of Mansell Street, turned left on to Aldgate High Street, and disappeared from view. With my heart in my throat, and the bottle of holy water in my hand, I quickened my step. I reached the end of the street and looked right to find the man had disappeared. Then, as a marked police van raced down Aldgate High Street from my right, I saw the man dart into the entrance of Aldgate tube station. Careful not to be hit by a night bus, I raced across the road and towards the front of the underground station.

"We have a suspect running on foot," an officer screeched through the scanner. Even though I knew they were talking about me, I couldn't give a shit. My sole focus was to catch up with that vampire. From over my shoulder, I heard a police van speed up as it came racing after me.

"*STOP!*" a voice hissed. It hadn't come from the scanner this time, but from the speakers on top of the police van.

I ran on, the entrance to the tube station only yards away now. I was so close, and nothing was going to stop me. I passed a rubbish bin and threw away the scanner. I didn't want to be caught with that. Pockets stuffed with cloves of garlic and a bottle of holy water would be hard enough to explain away if I were to be caught, but a police scanner was illegal and I would be in all kinds of shit.

The station concourse was empty, apart from a tired-looking ticket collector who stood by the barriers. They were closed, and I fumbled about in my coat pocket for my Oyster card. The sound of screeching tyres was almost deafening as the police van stopped outside the entrance to the station. Glancing over my shoulder, I could see the side door fly open as several coppers clambered out. Each of them wore a military-style helmet, goggles, black overalls, and body armour. I gasped at the sight of the machine guns they carried in their hands.

"*Halt!*" one of them roared, aiming his gun at me.

With a sharp gasp, I looked front and bounded over the closed barrier line.

"Hey, lady!" the ticket inspector called after me. "You need a ticket to travel!"

I headed down the stairs, my boots making snapping

sounds which echoed all around me. There was a small over-bridge and I peered through the grating and down at the platforms. Both were deserted. Then I saw him, standing in the shadows at the end of the northbound platform.

With the sounds of the officers' boots thundering down the stairs behind me, I raced along the over-bridge and down onto the platform. I wanted them to follow me but not catch me, before reaching the man, the killer – the *vampire*. As I reached the platform, my long blond hair billowed back from my head as a tube train rattled out of the tunnel. It stopped, the doors slid open, and I watched the man quickly step from the shadows and onto the train. I knew that I wouldn't reach the front of the train before the doors closed or the cops got me. Darting onto the tube train via the nearest set of open doors, I looked back to see the armed officers charge onto the platform.

"There she is!" one of them barked, raising his gun.

Not wasting any time, I turned and ran through the empty carriage. There was a beeping noise as the doors slid closed. I glanced back over my shoulder and could see one of the officers racing alongside the train on the platform, his gun trained on me.

"Stop the train! Stop the train!" he was shouting.

The train pulled away, and I watched the cops who were left behind on the platform. One of them started to bark into his radio. I looked up at the tube map attached to the carriage wall and could see the next stop was Liverpool Street. I knew that's where they would stop the train. Knowing that I only had minutes to reach the vampire, I turned and raced through the carriage. Reaching the interconnecting carriage door, I yanked it open and paused. For as long as I could remember, I had wanted to prove the existence of vampires and I never truly knew why. But now, as I was about to fulfil my lifelong dream, I was scared. It was like the realisation of what I was doing – what I was about to find – hit me, like driving your car head-on into a wall.

With my heart racing and my stomach doing somersaults, I closed the door behind me and stepped into the next carriage. The lights flickered off, sending me into darkness. I gasped and gripped the bottle of holy water. The lights came back on and I peered ahead, searching for the vampire in the empty carriage. I couldn't see him. With the train rocking from side to side, I made my way slowly forward. When I reached the end of the coach, I peered through the glass window in the connecting doors. The next carriage looked empty, too. Where was he? Was he on the train? Had he managed to give the cops and me the slip, sliding back into the shadows at the end of the platform? Would those cops have even noticed him? They seemed too intent on chasing me.

The train rattled through the tunnel, its lights flickering

on and off, leaving me in darkness for moments that seemed to last an eternity.

"Hello?" I called out. Now why did I do that? Did I really think he would suddenly appear with a big smile and ask me how I was doing? I did it because I was scared and couldn't bear the sound of my own heart beating frantically with fear inside my chest.

I reached the last adjoining door. There was only one carriage left. Knowing that if the vampire hadn't given me the slip and was still on the train he had to be inside this one, I slowly opened the interconnecting door. The train lurched left and right as it raced over points in the tunnel. With only minutes to go before we reached Liverpool Street Station, I scanned the carriage. Like the others, it was empty. Half of me felt cheated that I had come so close, but there was another part of me that sighed with relief. Even so, I had to make sure. So, unscrewing the lid from the bottle of holy water, I made my way down the gangway and passed the rows of seats. I glanced back over my shoulder and the other carriages snaked vacantly behind me.

With my heart racing so fast inside my chest I thought it might just go *bang*, I faced front again. Then I jumped as I saw a brief reflection of someone in the window. For just a second, I thought there was a pale-faced man inside the tunnel, but my skin turned cold as I realised he was standing right behind me. Before I had a chance to react, he had grabbed me. With his arm wrapped about my throat, I struggled, gasping for breath. His coat smelt old and musty.

"Why are you following me?" he breathed in my ear, and his breath felt ice-cold against my cheek.

With my knees just wanting to buckle beneath me with fear, I said, "I know what you are."

"And what is that?" he whispered, my neck breaking out in gooseflesh.

"You're a vampire," I gasped, his arm tightening about my throat. I struggled against him, trying to twist my neck to the right so I could see his face. With his free hand, he ran one long, white, bony finger down the length of my cheek. His fingernail felt like a blade.

"Oh, Sammy, you don't remember," he said softly in my ear.

"How do you know my name?" I asked numbly, raising the bottle of holy water.

"How quickly you have forgotten," he teased, and his breath smelt as stale and old as his coat.

The lights flickered out again, and seizing my chance, I jerked my arm backwards, throwing the holy water into his face. I heard him chuckle softly, and the lights came back on.

"Sammy, you really don't know who I am, do you?" he said. Although I couldn't see his face, I knew he was smiling, and that smile was full of pointed teeth. "Holy water doesn't work, nor does the garlic I can smell in your pocket, or the crucifix which glistens between your breasts."

"What have I forgotten?" I wheezed, as his grip became almost suffocating.

"Let me show you," he whispered as the train rattled into Liverpool Street Station and the carriage filled with bright white light . . .

2

. . . The light was intense. I immediately covered my eyes with my hands. It was hot, too – like the hottest summer's day. But there was something else. I was lying down on my back and the ground was hard. There was a breeze, but it did nothing to cool the extreme heat. Slowly, I lowered my hands and squinted up at the bright white sun that shone down from above. I was looking up into the palest of blue skies. Wisps of cloud covered it like white scars. My throat felt dry, as if I had swallowed broken glass. Something warm and sticky trickled down the side of my face and I gently dabbed at it with my fingertips. I pulled them away and they were smeared red.

"Get up!" someone snapped, and grabbed my arm. Their grip was so tight that a bolt of pain exploded up my arm and it made me feel sick.

I was pulled to my feet, and opening my eyes, I looked down to see the corpses of four men lying at my feet. Their faces were upturned, and each of them had an angry-looking hole in their foreheads.

"You'll pay for what you did," the voice hissed again, and I turned in the direction of it.

A weather-beaten face of a man stared into mine. His skin looked leathery and orange as if he had fallen asleep for several days on a sunbed. Black whiskers protruded from his chin like needles, and a set of wiry black eyebrows dropped over his piercing eyes.

"Look what you did to my men!" he barked, and I could see that his top two front teeth were nothing more than rotten stumps.

I glanced down at the four dead men again and whispered, "Did I do that?" It wasn't only the sight of the dead men I found confusing, but the way in which they were all dressed. They looked like cowboys. Each of them wore faded brown trousers which looked as if they had been cut from a rough cloth. They wore filthy-looking shirts which were tied up at the front with some kind of string. On their feet they wore leather boots, and around their hips and thighs were fastened holsters.

"What's going on?" I asked wearily, feeling as if I had just woken from the worst hangover ever.

"You killed my men," the man said again. Looking back at him, I could see that he was dressed just like the others. Then, without warning, he rolled back his fist and smashed it into the bony part of my skull, just between my eyes. My head rocked back, and I lost my footing. I hit the ground, sending up a plume of sand and dust. My brain felt as if it had been hacked away at with an ice pick. Then, as if my instincts were taking over, I reached for my . . .

"Looking for these?" the man asked, with a bemused chuckle.

Opening my eyes, I peered up at him, and could see that he was holding two gleaming guns in his hands. They looked as if they were made of silver, with smooth, wooden handles. Were they really mine? I wondered. I'd never owned a gun before. But something inside of me wanted to reach out for them, snatch them from him, and hold them in my hands. I could sense how they would feel in my fists, just the right weight, their smooth, sandalwood handles fitting the inside of my hands like gloves. I stared up at him, and all at once I could see how I could get them, even though I was on my back and he towered over me.

The man in the odd-looking cowboy outfit pointed the guns down at me, and the sun winked on and off them, reflecting against the silver barrel. "I've a good mind to kill you right now for what you've done, you filthy whore, but first I'm gonna have me some fun."

He holstered one of the guns, and with his free hand, he started to loosen the knotted length of string that held his trousers in place. He wobbled awkwardly as he tried to free himself from the front of his trousers and I knew that I was in the crap. The gun wavered from side to side with excitement. I looked up at him, the whole time my aching brain telling me how I could still get out if this. It was like my mind belonged to someone else – to someone who knew how to fight, someone who could handle themselves.

With his free hand disappearing into the front of his trousers, he looked down at me, and with his tongue running over his two broken teeth, he smiled and said, "Strip."

Before I'd the chance to say anything, I heard a voice from above me.

"Now that's no way to treat a lady," the voice said.

The man with the gun and his hand down the front of his trousers stopped trying to work himself free and glanced up. Cocking my head to one side in the sand and dust, I looked up to see what appeared to be a priest standing on a small ledge of rock behind me. He was dressed in black from his boots to the wide-brimmed hat he wore on his head. The only colour was the white dog collar about his throat and the droopy white moustache which covered his top lip.

"This has nothing to do with you, preacher," the man said, and spat a ball of phlegm into the sand at the foot of the rocks. Then, pointing his gun up at the priest, he added: "Now, why don't you go on your way."

"Now, I'm just a simple man of the cloth," the priest said, and his voice was soft, as if he was praying rather than talking. "I can see that you know how to handle a gun, so I'm not looking for any trouble. So just hand the girl over to me and I shall be on my way."

"Hand the girl over to you?" the man sneered, taking his hand from the front of his trousers and rubbing the hairs on his chin. "I tell you what, preacher man – this young girl ain't no God-fearing sort. She is a born killer – that's what she is."

"She looks like a scared child to me," the preacher said, the tails of his long black coat flapping in the warm breeze.

"Did you see what she did to my men?" the man barked, gesturing at the corpses with his free hand. "She killed all of 'em. Never seen a woman shoot a gun like that before. No, Father, you pass right on by and let me send her straight back to Hell."

"I can't do that," the preacher said. "Like the story in the Bible, I can't just pass on by."

Training his gun on the priest, the man said, "And I know my Bible, Father, and the priest in that story passed right on by – so why don't you do the same."

"Because I ain't no priest," the man in black said, and before I knew what had happened, he had drawn a gun into each hand and was pointing them down at the man. It happened so quickly, the two gleaming pistols appeared in his hands as if by magic.

A look of confusion passed over the man's face. As if my mind was taken hostage again by another, I watched as if in slow motion as his finger pressed down on the trigger. Then I was up, off my back and pouncing through the air. The man saw me from the corner of his eye and turned, but I was too quick and before either of us truly knew what was happening, my left elbow had connected with his jaw. His head snapped to the left, the gun flying from his fist. As if functioning on some kind of autopilot, I had snatched the gun out of the air, cocked it, and shot the man in the face. He flew backwards through the air as if hit by a cannonball instead of a bullet. His brains exploded out the back of his head like a lump of raw hamburger. Before he had hit the ground, I had bent down, snatched my other gun from his holster, and was pointing both of them at the preacher, who stood on the lip of red-coloured rock above me.

With my arms locked rigidly before me and with my heart racing, I looked at the preacher and stared into the piercing blue eyes that twinkled beneath the rim of his hat.

"Did you see what I just did?" I asked him.

"Very impressive," he said, re-holstering his own guns beneath the folds of his long coat.

"I wasn't looking for praise," I breathed. "What I meant was – did you see what I just did? I can't do stuff like that."

"You just did," he said, his thick white moustache twitching as he spoke.

"I killed all of these men," I gasped, lowering my guns and looking down at the dead spread out at my feet. "Why did I do that?"

"Because they were going to hurt you, I reckon," the priest said dryly. Then, disappearing behind the rock, he reappeared moments later, leading the sleekest-looking horse I had ever seen. Its coat and mane were jet-black and seemed to shimmer like silver beneath the overpowering glare of the sun.

"Where's your horse?" the priest asked, staring at me.

"Horse?" I breathed. "I was on a train."

"A train you say?" the priest said, sounding bemused and pulling the brim of his hat down over his eyes. "The nearest railroad is ten miles away, back in the town of Black Water Gap."

"How far am I from Aldgate?" I asked him.

"Never heard of it, little lady," he said, turning his horse, its long black tail swishing away a swarm of flies.

"I can take you to Crows Ranch," he offered, looking back over his shoulder at me.

"Where am I? This isn't London, is it?" I asked him, my head pounding and feeling lost and disorientated. "What year is this?"

"No, this isn't London, and the year?" he half-smiled

20

beneath his moustache, "It's 1888 and I've got me some Vrykolakas to catch."

"Vrykolakas?" I asked, feeling dizzy.

"Vampires, my dear child, *vampires*," the priest smiled.

Unable to support me any longer, my knees gave way, and I collapsed, the new world I found myself in turning black before me.

3

The black changed to grey then back to black again. I felt so tired and my head still hurt. I just wanted to sleep. So I did. But in the darkness I could hear voices and the sound of wheels rattling over a rough and uneven terrain.

"Who is she?" one of the voices asked in a hushed whisper.

"Dunno," another said, and it sounded familiar. "But she sure knows how to handle a gun."

The world seemed to lurch, jolt, then right itself again. I wanted to open my eyes to see who it was that was speaking. My eyelids felt so heavy, as if being held down by two invisible thumbs. So I slipped back down into the darkness and let it wrap itself around me like a thick coat. But the voices continued, each one of them just above a whisper.

"Where did she come from?"

"I don't know that either, but she moved with the agility and speed of a cat," the voice said again, and in the dark I saw a priest, his white collar shining out of the black.

Wheels spinning beneath me and the smell of dust and old leather stirred me from my sleep – *nightmare.*

"How fast was she?" someone asked the priest.

"Fast!" came his hushed reply. "She killed five men. The last of them didn't know his brains were flying out the back of his head 'til he was lying on his ass, twitching and jerking."

In my dream-like state, I remembered arriving in the desert. . .

. . .The wind was warm like the heat from the hairdryer in my flat. There was something on my head – it was a wide-brimmed hat – dark brown and made of leather. I wore a dark grey top, rough woven jeans, boots, and a long brown coat. As I watched the coat tails flap about my legs in the breeze, I wondered where I was and why I was a dressed like a cowboy – cowgirl?

Hadn't I just been on a tube train? I wondered, my mind racing. There had been someone else, a man. His arm had been tight about my throat. A vampire! But where was I now? This wasn't London. This wasn't Liverpool Street Tube Station, right?

I looked around me, and for as far as I could see, the

ground stretched away on a flat and even plain. It was cracked, as if it hadn't felt rain upon it for years. Puffs of dust blew up into the air, and in the distance I could hear the sound of a buzzard screeching. There were thick, dried-out-looking shrubs sticking up from the ground. Then, in the distance, I could see a row of shapes moving towards me. They appeared to shimmer in the heat – but as they drew closer, I could see they were people and they were coming towards me on horses.

Maybe they could help me? I wondered. Perhaps they could tell me where I was?

With the wind and the dust blowing around me, I held my hand over my eyes to block out the glare of the sun and watched the riders come towards me. The horses' hooves kicked out clouds of grit and dirt and the sound of them was like thunder rolling across the desert. As the riders drew nearer, I could see that there were five men. Each of them wore clothes similar in style to mine. Watching them, I got a feeling in my stomach that something was wrong – everything was wrong with this picture.

They reached me, and each of their faces was filthy-looking, worn, dark brown, and wrinkled by the desert sun. Sweat ran down the front and back of their shirts in "V" shapes. All of them had guns strapped to their thighs.

"What have we here?" the first of them said as he circled me on his horse. Beads of sweat glistened on

his brow and he armed it away with the sleeve of his blue shirt. His voice was rough. But it was his eyes; they never met mine but just looked me up and down like I was standing before him naked.

"Whoo-hoo!" another seemed to cheer with excitement, and slapped the neck of his horse with the flat of his hand. The horse trotted forward a few steps and flicked its long brown tail.

"Can you help me?" I asked them.

"Sure we can help you," the man with the sweat running from his brow said, dismounting from his horse. The others followed.

"It's just that I'm not sure where I am or how I got here," I said, taking a step backwards and away from them.

"Poor little thing is lost," another of the men laughed. This one seemed to be chewing on something that he had placed inside the cheek of his mouth. He grinned at me, but it wasn't friendly. He then spat a jet of brown liquid from the corner of his mouth and the ground greedily soaked it up.

The first of them came behind me and I felt myself go tense. His breath was hot against my cheek and it stank of sour whiskey. Taking a strand of my hair in his hands, he sniffed at it.

"Sweet," I heard him breathe.

Another of them came towards me, and my heart began to pound in my chest. This guy had two broken

25

front teeth, probably knocked out in a fight. There were just two broken stumps, which were more yellow than white, and they protruded from gums which looked raw and infected.

There was a part of me that just wanted to run from them, but there was another part – a newer part – that was already figuring out how I could kill these men, should I need to. My eyes flickered between them, working out the distance each of them was from me, their height, and where their guns were.

"Look, I just want to go home," I said to the one with the broken teeth.

"There ain't no rush," he grinned. "Let's have ourselves a little party."

"I'm not in the mood for a party," I said flatly, and even though it was my voice, it was like it had come from that other part of me.

The cowboy's eyes widened just a fraction as if surprised by my lack of fear. Then without warning, he reached out with his hand and roughly gripped my left breast. A spike of pain shot into my shoulder blade. As quickly as he had grabbed me, I had seized his wrist and yanked his hand away.

"Don't touch me," I told him, staring straight into his eyes.

Trying to mask his own surprise at how quickly I had removed his hand, he turned to his friends and laughing, he said, "Boys, it looks as if we have a wild one here!"

"The wilder, the better!" the one who had slapped his horse whooped with excitement.

The man behind me suddenly grabbed my throat, snaked his arm around my waist and shoved his hard-on into the small of my back. Then, all hell broke loose. Jerking my right hand backwards, I gripped the man's genitals and twisted my wrist and pulled. He made a deafening scream in my ear, and I felt him drop. The male with the rotten gums lurched for me, and I snapped my head forward, my brow connecting with the bridge of his nose. I heard a cracking sound as he flew backwards, his hands to his face. The other three by the horses reached for their guns. There were several deep booming sounds and all three of them were flying backwards through the air, their heads erupting in a shower of red mess. Wondering where the gunfire had come from, I looked down to see I was holding two gleaming handguns. Smoke trailed from the barrels in wispy streams.

How had they gotten there? I wondered. But before I'd had the chance to consider my own question, I heard a voice from behind me.

"You fucking whore!" the voice screeched.

I spun around to see the guy holding his crotch with one hand and reaching for his gun with the other. Before I truly knew what had happened, a deep, black hole the size of a large coin had opened up in his forehead and the gun was thundering in my fist again. A crimson

27

*jet of blood squirted from his mouth and he flopped
onto his side, the hand that was still holding his groin
twitching, as if he had died messing with himself. Fretful,
the horses whinnied, reared up on their hind legs, and
galloped away. Then, I felt a pain in the back of my
head, and I crumpled to the hard-packed ground, my
guns spilling from my hands. I peered up into the sun
and could see the man with the broken teeth swaying
before me and everything went black again. . .*

. . .In the darkness I could hear those voices again, as
if they were coming from far away, hushed and ghost-
like.

"She's English," the preacher said.

"How do you know?" asked another.

"Her accent – and she asked if she was in London,"
he said.

"London?" a voice cut in, this one female. "A long
way from home then?"

"We could use her – replace Marley," another voice
spoke. "If she is as quick on the draw like you say she
is, then . . . "

"No one could replace Marley," another voice broke
into the darkness. "She could never be replaced."

"You should have thought of that before . . . " the
preacher started and the blackness took me again, his
voice fading away.

4

I woke to find myself in some kind of covered wagon. I was stretched out on a narrow, leather-covered bench and my feet hung over the end. It was dark and the only light came from an oil lamp which hung from the roof of the wagon. It wasn't as hot as I had remembered it to be, but it wasn't cold, either. I looked down the length of my body and could see that I was dressed in the same clothes that I had been wearing in my dream.

But had it been a dream? I wondered. I was beginning to fear not. In my head I could hear that man – the preacher – telling me that it was the year 1888. That was the last thing I had heard before collapsing into unconsciousness. Swinging my legs over the side of the bench, I wondered how and why I was back in the year 1888 – that is, if I really was. I had been in London, chasing down that man – the one they called the Jack the Ripper copycat. But he hadn't been any Ripper copycat, he had been a vampire and I had been close to proving it.

I touched my neck where he had gripped me with his arm, and just for a second, I felt his ice-cold breath on my cheek. Who had he been and where was he now? If I was truly back in 1888, was he here, too? The flaps of material which covered the opening to the wagon fluttered like two sails. I wondered if I opened them, would I be back in London, just like Lucy opening the wardrobe door and stepping out of Narnia and back into her own world – her own reality? I stood up and felt something slap against my thighs. Looking down I could see those two giant pistols in leather holsters. Just a figment of my imagination, like the Turkish Delight the White Witch had given Edmund back in Narnia. But they felt real, the smell of gunpowder smelt real enough – but it had to be my imagination. I was probably unconscious on the London Underground, going around and around on the Circle Line, where that man had left me.

I reached for the flaps and knew that as soon as I pulled them back, I would find myself back on that tube train, surrounded by armed police officers. Taking a deep breath, I closed my eyes and yanked back the flaps of material hanging over the entrance to the wagon. With my eyes still shut, I listened. I could hear voices.

Cops, just like I knew there would be. Opening my eyes, I looked out and gasped. The night sky was black and star-shot. I had never seen so many stars before. They looked so clear and bright and there were thousands of them. The sky had never looked this perfect before – not in London, anyhow.

I glanced down from the sky and followed the sound of the voices. There was a fire burning, and sitting around it were four people. The orange glow of the fire gave them a warm ghostly look. One of them looked up and I recognised him from my dream. The preacher – or was he a priest? He was taller than I remembered him, standing at least six-foot-four tall. He was slim, and without the dark-brimmed hat I remembered him to wear, his hair was black and cut short. At the front, he had a streak of hair that was snow white, a bit like a skunk. In the glow of the fire, his eyes were still a sharp blue and seemed to cut right through me. That white-coloured moustache drooped down over his top lip like a bike handlebar, and matched the blaze of white hair that streaked back from his brow. Despite his white moustache, behind it, I could see that he wasn't that old, no more than forty.

"Come and join us," he said, gesturing me forward with a strong-looking hand.

I didn't say anything and I looked at the others who had all turned to stare at me. There were two women and another man.

"You have nothing to fear," the preacher called. "Please come and join us. We have elk soup and chilli beans in the pot."

What's elk? I wondered. *Or did he say elf?* This shit just keeps getting crazier and crazier. I really must have banged my head hard, back in 2012.

"Please," one of the women said, smiling back at me. From where I was standing, I was struck by her prettiness. Her long black hair and dark brown eyes reflected the flames from the fire. "Come and warm yourself."

I climbed down from the back of the wagon, and with each of their eyes on me; I made my way towards the fire. Hunkering down, I crossed my legs and sat down next to the pretty-looking woman who had spoken to me.

"I'm Louise Pearson," she said, offering me a smile.

Sitting so close to her, I could see she was in her early thirties, with raven black hair which she had pulled into a ponytail at the base of her neck. It was fixed in place with a piece of leather string. She wore a beige-coloured blouse, which was open at the throat, and blue trousers similar to jeans, which were flared at the bottom. Like my own feet, hers were covered in a scuffed pair of boots. Over the blouse, Louise wore a faded sleeveless black jacket, similar to a waistcoat. Strapped to her thighs were two revolvers. The barrels were so long that they nearly reached her knees.

Before I'd had a chance to say anything, the other

woman, who was seated next to Louise, spoke. "My name's Zoe Edgar. The preacher has told us all about you."

"Has he?" I said, glancing across the fire at him. I wondered what he knew about me.

"He said you are English and come from London. Is that true?" she asked, her voice sounding kind of excited.

"I guess," I whispered, looking at her, still unable to comprehend how I'd come to be sitting around a campfire dressed as a cowgirl and talking to a group of people who should have long since died.

"You don't sound too sure," Zoe came back, her green eyes sparkling in the light of the fire. She was no older than eighteen, and like Louise, she was real pretty. Her hair was dark blond and shoulder length. She had a really infectious smile that looked as if she was about to burst into a sudden fit of the giggles at any moment.

"So what's England like?" Zoe asked, that excitement still brimming in her voice. Unlike Louise, she wore a long velvet dress. But she had guns, which hung beneath her arms in a set of holsters.

"Erm . . ." I started, not knowing what to say.

"Leave her be," the preacher cut in and saved me. "The girl has had a nasty knock to the head. Isn't that right?"

I looked at him and nodded.

"I was just curious, Preacher," she said, looking disappointed at him.

Ignoring her, the preacher turned and gestured towards the other man in the group. "This is Harrison."

I looked through the flames that licked the bottom of the pot hanging over the fire. Steam came from it, and the smell of elk or *elf* was sweet and intoxicating. My mouth began to water and my stomach rumbled. The man on the other side of the fire said something, but I had been too distracted by the food cooking before me.

"Sorry?" I said, taking my eyes off the pot. Then, truly seeing him for the first time, I wondered how I had ever been distracted by the simmering pot of food. He could have only been a few years older than me, making him about twenty-five, but no older. He had light, sandy-brown hair, which was longer at the front than it was at the back. A flop of hair covered his brow. He had grey eyes, which had a hardness to them. The lower half of his face was covered with stubble, which made him look like he was cast in shadow. He had a firm jawline which looked as if it had been chipped from granite stone. Around his throat he wore a black bandana. His pale blue checked shirt was unbuttoned slightly and I could see the light from the fire glistening off a fine sheen of perspiration which covered his muscular chest. The sleeves of his shirt were rolled halfway up his thick forearms, and around the waist of his blue denims he wore a thick brown belt, from which hung his guns.

"Harry," he said, staring through the flames at me, his eyes cold and emotionless.

"Sorry?" I said again, and could have slapped myself for appearing like a dumb-arse.

"Harrison Turner, but people just call me Harry," he explained, his voice flat and deep.

"Oh, okay . . . sure," I mumbled.

Get a grip, Sammy, I scolded myself, but I was still having difficulty believing that I was sitting around a campfire in the middle of the desert, talking to real live cowgirls and cowboys – especially one as hot as the guy sitting opposite me.

"And you are?" he asked, hanging his forearms over his knees, his eyes never leaving mine. He might be hot but he was beginning to make me feel uncomfortable. Not in a creepy kind of way, but uncomfortable – like I was being studied by him.

I took a deep breath to gain some kind of composure and said, "My name is Samantha Carter, but like you, everyone calls me Sammy."

"No one calls me Sammy," he said flatly.

"You know what I mean," I shot back. He had pissed me off now. Then, realising I wasn't just hungry but was craving something else, I looked at the others and asked, "Does anyone here smoke?"

Louise and Zoe looked at the preacher. I watched as he pulled a small wooden box from his coat pocket. He opened it, took out what looked like a cigarette, and passed it to me. Taking it between my fingers, I could see it had been hand-rolled. I popped it between my lips as the preacher struck a match and held it to the end of my cigarette. I drew in deeply, and the smoke hit the back of my throat. It was hot and strong – not like the cigarettes I was used to. I doubted they had filtered tips and extra lights here. With tears streaming from my eyes, I coughed and spluttered the smoke from the back of my throat.

"Do you actually smoke?" the preacher asked, hitting the area between my shoulder blades with the flat of his hand.

"Way more than is good for me," I choked. I glanced across the fire and could see a half-smile tugging at the corners of Harry's lips. *Arsehole*, I thought to myself. The good-looking ones always were.

Once I had gotten to grips with the coughing fit, I let the cigarette dangle between my fingers, taking just the smallest of puffs every now and then. I didn't want to amuse Harry any further.

"Let's eat," Louise said, picking up a stack of tin plates which were on the ground beside her. She handed them around, while Zoe gave out forks. Louise removed the lid from the pot which hung over the fire. A waft of steam belched up into the night and disappeared. The smell of the food was wonderful and my stomach knotted. I couldn't remember when I had last eaten. I knew it had to have been back in London, and knowing my love of fast food, it had probably been a Big Mac. No more Big Macs, large fries, and chocolate milkshakes for me – not for another seventy years or so, if I truly was in the late 1800's. Louise ladled a heap of the stew and chilli beans onto my plate, and to be honest, it smelt way better than any burger I had ever eaten.

I forked some of the stew into my mouth and started coughing all over again. The beans were very hot in flavour, and my tongue burnt as if I had just drank a bottle of Tabasco sauce. With my eyes watering and my nose running, I turned away so Harry couldn't take delight in my suffering again.

"Water," I heard the preacher say.

While I held my throat with my free hand, someone thrust a small flask at me. I looked up to see Harry towering over me. I took the flask and gulped from it, hoping that the water would soothe my throat. But it wasn't water and Harry knew it. The whiskey washed over my tongue, almost scalding the inside of my mouth. The taste mixed with the chilli beans took my breath away and I gasped and spluttered. With my eyes red-rimmed, and snot streaming from my nose, I stared up at Harry.

"You dick . . ." I started.

"No, *Harry*," he half-smiled again.

"I said give the girl water, Harry," the preacher snapped, rushing towards me. "Not whiskey!"

37

"Oh, shit," Harry said, taking the flask from me, his grey eyes now twinkling. "I gave her the wrong . . ."

But before he could finish, Zoe was kneeling beside me and thrusting a leather-bound canteen into my free hand. "Drink some of this," she urged.

I placed it against my lips, tilted my head back, and gulped down the water. It was cold, and it cooled the inside of my mouth, washing away the taste of the whiskey and chilli. Handing the canteen back to Zoe, I thanked her and watched Harry sit down by the fire again.

He looked at me, shrugged his shoulders, and said, "Sorry, it was an honest mistake."

"Whatever," I scowled. I pushed the beans to the edge of my plate and forked up some of the stew.

"Are you all right?" Louise asked around a mouthful of the beans.

"No, not really," I said, without looking up, not wanting to make eye contact with Harry. He wasn't hot – he was a dickhead.

"What's wrong?" Zoe asked, and her voice was soft, like she really cared.

Placing my food to one side, I looked at her and said, "I shouldn't be here. None of you are real – you can't be. I'm from another place, another time, and I want to go back."

Then, moving faster than I could blink, the four of them were standing before me, their guns drawn.

5

As quickly as they had drawn their guns, I had drawn mine, and I was standing. My arms were locked straight out in front. They looked at me, never once taking their eyes from the revolvers that I had pointed on them. Again, I was surprised at the speed in which I had sprung to my feet and drawn my weapons.

"You were right, Preacher," Harry said, keeping his eyes on me. "She is quick."

"Perhaps too quick," Louise said, her guns not wavering an inch.

"Is she a Vrykolakas?" Zoe asked, that smile of hers now a thin line, like a slash across the lower half of her face.

I'd heard the preacher say that word before, and it meant vampire.

"I'm not a vampire," I said, looking into the preacher's eyes.

"You said you were from another time," he reminded me, matching my stare. "How old are you, exactly?"

"I'm twenty-two," I told him.

"When were you born?" he came back at me, forefinger hovering over his trigger.

"London, England," I said straight back.

"He asked, *when*, not *where*," Harry snapped, and I heard the click of the hammer going back on his gun.

Now mathematics had never been one of my strong points, but my intuition wasn't as bad, and something told me that if I told them I had been born in 1990, I was going to be in the crap. So as quickly as I could, I tried to take twenty-two from eighty-eight.

"I was born in 1866," I told them.

"What are you doing here?" Louise asked, the guns still trained on me.

"I was hoping that perhaps you could tell me that," I half-smiled.

"What's that s'posed to mean?" Harry snapped.

Knowing I had to start explaining – and fast, or otherwise they would probably suspect me of being a vampire and shoot me, I said, "It's all kind of confusing, really. But back home, in London, there was this killer. The police thought he was a man and they called him 'Jack the Ripper', but I wasn't so sure. I thought he was something different altogether."

40

"Like what?" the preacher asked, his eyes narrowing beneath his white eyebrows.

"Well, it's kind of like this," I started to explain. "Each of the victims had their throats slashed and they were all drained of blood. Now, I guess like you," and I raised an eyebrow at them, "I have an interest in vampires. So I tracked this one down. I followed him onto a train, but he caught me . . ."

"Did he bite you?" Zoe cut in, that excitement back in her voice again.

"No," I said.

"How did you get away?" Louise asked, and I could sense a note of suspicion in her voice.

"Now this is where it all gets a bit hazy," I said, choosing my words with care. "He gripped me around the throat and I blacked out. The next thing I knew, I was here in the desert and the rest you know," I said, looking over at the preacher.

"You said you were on a train, what train?" he asked, and this seemed to interest him somehow.

"A train back home in London," I said. Now that wasn't a lie.

"A steam train?" Harry asked.

"You got it," I said back. This was a lie, but how could I explain we had electric trains which ran beneath the ground? Did they even have electricity in 1888? My history was as bad as my math.

"That still doesn't explain how you have ended up

on the other side of the world," Louise said, the fire crackling behind her.

"Like I've already told you, I don't know how I got to be here either," I replied. "Maybe one day I'll remember – figure it out – because if I do, then maybe I can go home, back to . . . " I was just about to say 2012, when I stopped myself and said, "London."

"It doesn't add up," Harry said, glancing at the preacher, his guns still aimed at me.

"The preacher said that I had been hit hard on the head," I reminded them. "Perhaps I'm suffering from amnesia."

"What's that?" Zoe cut in.

"Loss of memory," I explained. "But one thing I am sure of is that I'm no vampire or whatever it is you call them."

Slowly, the preacher lowered his guns, but didn't holster them. "You said that you were interested in vampires. Why?" he asked me, from beneath that white moustache.

"Why not?" I shot back. "You seem to be more than interested in them yourselves."

"They've killed here, just like you say they have in your London," he explained. "We hunt them."

"Like bounty hunters, you mean?" thinking of the westerns I'd seen as a kid on TV.

"Not like bounty hunters," Harry cut in, his eyes glinting like two chinks of grey flint. "We're more than that."

42

"So you all have jobs then?" I asked, trying not to sound flippant, but there was a part of me that still wondered if this was all really happening. Maybe I would wake up at any moment, going round and round on that tube train until the cops found me and woke me up.

"We can be hired from time to time," Harry said.

"For what?"

"This and that," Zoe answered.

"Protection," the preacher said, and now he did holster his guns, suggesting he believed my story and no longer suspected me of being a threat to him and his friends. Unlike him, the others persisted in aiming their guns at me.

"Protection from what?" I asked him, putting my own guns away and sitting back down before the fire.

"The vampires," the preacher said, taking up his plate again and forking beans into his mouth. "We've killed some of them, but there are plenty of them left, hiding in mines and caves in the mountains.

"So people believe vampires exist here?" I asked him, knowing that back home, people didn't really believe in such things.

"No, not all of them," Harry answered for the preacher, his guns still drawn. "That's the problem. People are blind to what they don't believe in. That's how the vampires have gotten away with their killing for so long."

I thought of the killer from home – my home in 2012 – and knew that they would never catch the killer because they didn't believe. They were looking for a man – not a monster. Although it pained me to admit that Harry was right, he was bang-on. The police back home laughed at the idea of a vampire committing the killings and that's why he would continue to slip through their fingers. They couldn't see what they didn't believe in.

"So why do you believe?" I asked Harry, as the preacher gestured to him and the others to lower their guns.

Taking his place back around the fire, Harry said, "We believe because we've all lost someone to those creatures. We've seen what they can do. We've seen what happened to those we cared about – we saw what they became."

"What about you?" Louise asked me, scrapping the remains of her food from the plate and into the fire. The flames hissed and spat.

"What about me?" I said.

"Why do you believe in vampires?"

I sat thoughtfully for a moment, not knowing what to say. Where had my interest – my unwavering belief that vampires existed – come from? It had always been there – but why? Looking at Louise's pretty face through the flames, I said, "I don't know."

"Something else you've forgotten?" Harry muttered.

"Perhaps," I whispered.

An uncomfortable silence fell over us and I sat and wondered if they truly believed what I had said or not. But did it really matter? They were all probably a part of my subconscious as I lay unconscious on the floor of that tube train, waiting for the police to find me. But would I be able to create something so real? The smell of the food, the taste of those chilli beans – it all felt so real. Would my subconscious be able to conjure up all that stuff? And why the old west and the year 1888? If I were unconscious back in London of 2012 – why would I have dreamt something like this up? Why dream about a cowboy with attitude, two pretty cowgirls with guns, and a preacher who perhaps wasn't even a preacher? I had no interest in the old west. But if it was all real, if this wasn't a nightmare I was creating on the floor of that tube train – why was I here?

With the sound of the fire burning before us, the preacher poked at it with a twig, and looking through the flames at me, he said, "Tell me about the man on the train – this Jack the Ripper."

6

I had studied the Ripper case – what student criminologist hadn't? Some of them had been so obsessed by the case it had become their life's work, calling themselves Ripperologists. Why? He was the first recorded serial killer and all criminologists wanted to study one of them. And the fact that Jack had never been caught just added fuel to the flames of the conspiracy theories which had been created. To truly discover the identity of Jack the Ripper was the Holy Grail of criminology.

But how did I answer the preacher's question? He was asking me about the guy – the one I suspected of being a vampire – from 2012, not the infamous Ripper who had stalked the backstreets of Whitechapel in the London of 1888. The guy on the tube train wasn't the

Ripper, he was someone completely different. But it was him that the preacher wanted to know about, because I was connected to him – he was the person who had sent me here.

They sat silently, looking at me through the flames, waiting for me to talk. It had turned cold, and I pulled the long brown coat that I was wearing tight about me. The sky was like a sheet of black glass that had been sprinkled with silver glitter. Apart from the sound of the wood snapping in the fire before me, the only other noise I could hear was the neighing of their horses.

The preacher took two more of those hand-rolled cigarettes from the box and lit both of them. One he stuck in the corner of his mouth, and the other he passed to me. I took a puff, careful not to draw too heavily on it. I didn't want another coughing fit. With a wisp of grey smoke curling up from the corner of my mouth, I looked at the group huddled around the fire and said, "Jack the Ripper was responsible for the deaths of five women. He was called other names like 'Leather Apron' and 'The Whitechapel Murderer', but it was the 'Ripper' name that stuck."

"Why Ripper?" the preacher asked, the end of his cigarette winking on and off in the dark.

"He ripped open his victims' throats, stomachs, removed their internal organs, and mutilated their faces and genitals," I told them.

"So this is the vampire that you were following?"

Harry asked, his eyes fixed on me, as if studying my every movement. "They called this vampire *Jack the Ripper* where you come from?"

I wanted to tell him no, that it wasn't the Ripper, but how did I explain? How did I explain I was chasing after someone who the press had referred to as a 'Jack the Ripper copycat killer', that it was only me who suspected him of being a vampire? If I told them the truth, Harry and his friends would be facing off with me again, suspecting me of being a vampire, too. But did it really matter what I told them? They weren't real – none of this was. The only reason I was sitting here discussing Jack the Ripper was because my unconscious mind was scrambling through all the information in my head. A bit like going to sleep and dreaming about all the stuff you had done the previous day. The whole "Ripper" thing had been on my mind before I'd been strangled on that train, so it was reasonable, then, that my mind would be trying to make sense of it all. I would wake up any time now; those armed cops would be working on me, reviving me, blowing air into my lungs, pounding on my chest to give me a kick start. I was going to wake up at any moment.

So drawing on the cigarette again, I looked at Harry and said, "Yes, it was Jack the Ripper I was chasing. It was him who, I guess, brought me here."

"Why here?" Zoe asked, her eyes wide.

"Maybe he was close to being captured in London,"

Louise said thoughtfully. Then, turning to look at me she added, "You were chasing him, right? You caught up with him – you saw him – you could recognise him . . . "

"I never saw his face," I cut in. "He came at me from behind."

"That would explain why he didn't kill you like the others," Zoe added. "You didn't see his face."

Christ, they were reading more into this than I thought they would, I cursed myself. When is this going to stop? When am I going to wake up? Desperate to try and steer them away from the whole Ripper conspiracy thing, I said, "Look, none of this makes sense. How would he have travelled halfway around the world with me?"

"I thought you had an interest in vampires?" the preacher said.

"I do," I told him.

"Then you don't think it could be possible he could have brought you here? Vampires take on many forms. They can appear young or old, as mist or fog, and vanish in the blink of an eye. They can cross oceans of time – they have eternal life. He could have brought you here if it had been his wish to do so and you wouldn't necessarily remember or . . . "

"What did you say?" I cut in, my heart beginning to thump.

"That you needn't necessarily remember how he

brought you here, that would account for your loss of memory and . . . " the preacher started.

"No, not that," I snapped. "The crossing oceans of time thing."

"Vampires can live hundreds – thousands of years," the preacher explained. "They are not restricted by time like mortals are . . . "

The preacher's voice drifted away like the smoke curling up from the fire. *Oceans of time*, those words flooded my mind until they were almost deafening, and my heart raced. What if Jack the Ripper of 1888 was the vampire I had followed onto the London Underground in 2012? What if the preacher was right, that this vampire had crossed oceans of time, lived hundreds of years, and had come back to London one-hundred-and-twenty-four years later?

But what was I doing back in the old west in 1888?

Then as if in answer to my question, the preacher said, "You are not the only person from London who has recently arrived here."

"What do you mean?" I asked, peering at him.

"There is an English gentleman by the name of Spencer Drake who wishes to hire out our services," the preacher said, the cigarette poking out from beneath his white moustache. "He wants to meet with us tomorrow in the town of Black Water Gap."

"What does he want to hire you for?" I asked him.

"Not sure yet," he said, extinguishing his cigarette

between his thumb and forefinger. "But it's interesting, don't you think?" and he stared at me with his cold blue eyes.

"Sure," I whispered, and watched the preacher stand up.

"Tomorrow then," he said, stretching out his hand towards Louise. She stood, took his hand, and he led her towards the rear of the wagon. Once they were both inside, the preacher closed the flaps, sealing them both inside.

He definitely wasn't a preacher, I thought to myself.

Both Harry and Zoe got up. *Not them, too?* I wondered, but they only went to their horses and returned with what looked like rolls of blankets tucked under their arms. Harry rolled open the blanket and placed it on the ground a short distance from the fire. Without saying a word, he lay down on his side and closed his eyes. Zoe came around the fire towards me and handed me one of the blankets that she was carrying.

"Thank you, Zoe," I said, unrolling the blanket.

"That's okay," she smiled at me. I watched her settle down on the ground, pulling the rough-looking blanket up under her chin.

Lying on top of the blanket which she had given me, I tried to make myself as comfortable as possible. I pulled the collar of my coat up around my neck and lay on my back, looking up into the dead black sky.

"If it makes you feel any better, I never really believed that you were a vampire," Zoe suddenly whispered.

I rolled my head to one side and looked at her.

Looking at me from beneath a set of heavy eyelids, Zoe said, "There's something weird about you – but you're no vampire."

"How could you be so sure?" I whispered back.

"When you were unconscious in the back of that wagon the past few days, we found a handful of garlic in your pocket, a crucifix around your neck, and a bottle of holy water in your pocket."

Suddenly remembering how I had followed the killer down onto the Underground with my pockets full of these things, I looked at Zoe and said, "Where is my stuff now?"

"Marley threw it away," she whispered back.

I'd heard that name before. Hadn't I heard the preacher say that name as I had drifted in and out of consciousness in the back of the wagon? "Who's Marley?" I whispered back.

But before Zoe had the chance to answer me, Harry spoke in a gruff-sounding voice and said, "Zoe, that's enough already. Get some sleep."

Closing her eyes, Zoe rolled onto her side, turning her back towards me. I looked across the camp at Harry, but like Zoe, he had turned his back to me also.

As I lay in the dark, the glowing embers of the fire fading beside me, I tried to block out the sounds of the preacher's and Louise's humping. I thought of how many times I had overheard Sally and her boyfriends in the room next to mine in our flat back in London, and wondered why it was always me left lying awake in the dark listening to others enjoy themselves. As I tried not to listen to the preacher and Louise, I realised I had never heard such wild sounds before. Karl had never even brought me close to making noises like it. These cowboys and cowgirls obviously knew how to enjoy themselves.

I glanced quickly at Harry, his back towards me. Not wanting to even begin to contemplate what kind of lover he might be, I closed my eyes and wondered how long it would be before I could go home.

7

After only the briefest of conversations, he had struck the deal with the prostitute and the pair of them moved swiftly through the darkened streets. It was cold. The main street was busy with drunks who had stumbled out of the saloon. He wanted to keep away from them – other people. He was immaculately dressed in a long-tailed coat. She could see that he wore a crisp white collar and black tie about his throat. On his head he wore a hat that had a narrow brim and was round on top. The woman fancied that, despite his good looks and confident manner, he would be all over her in just a few minutes. That suited her, as she had a young one sleeping at home and she wanted to be out of the cold. The jeers and rants of the drunks faded into the distance, as the man led her off the main street and behind the shoesmith's. There was a building which looked similar in shape and size to a barn.

The man pressed his shoulder against the door and it creaked open. The barn smelt of animals, horses perhaps, but there were none present. He closed the door behind them, chinks of moonlight slicing through the gaps in the panelled walls. The man led the woman to the centre of the barn, and then with his foot, he brushed away the straw, making a circular clearing. The woman thought this was strange, as the straw would have been more comfortable to lie on while they carried out their business.

She ran a slender hand up and across his chest, opening the button with her fingernails, which were cracked and dirty.

"So what's your pleasure?" she said, trying to sound like she even gave a crap. She just wanted it over with.

"No talk," the man said, his voice deep and low.

She paused momentarily, and then continued. There was something about him she didn't like – but then again, she hadn't really liked any of the men she did business with. But this one was different. It was the way his eyes seemed to have no colour, like two white moons shining out of his face.

With hands that were trembling with the cold or fear – she couldn't be sure – she unfastened the rest of the buttons that held his expensive jacket together. That's why he doesn't want to get on the floor; he's worried he might spoil his . . .

"What are you wearing that for?" she suddenly gasped, opening his coat. Beneath it he was wearing an apron and it felt as if it were made from leather.

"Things might get messy," he said, his voice as deep as before.

"Hey, mister, I'm not into no . . . " but before she had a chance to finish, her head was swinging backwards on her neck like a hinge.

The man had moved with such speed that she had only seen the fleetest glimpse of what looked like a set of claws as they sliced through her throat. With her head hanging down her back, attached by the thinnest piece of flesh, she clawed blindly at her throat. To him, she looked as if she were trying to find her own head, so she could put it back on.

"Here, let me help you with that," he smiled, his voice barely audible over the sound of the gargling coming from the woman's neck.

Placing a long-fingered hand in the small of her back to steady the woman, the man lunged forward and bit through the sinew of flesh that was holding the woman's head in place. His razor-sharp teeth cut through the stringy lump of flesh as easy as if he were breaking cotton. Her head dropped and he caught it with his free hand. He raised it before his own face, and stared almost in wonder at the whites of her eyes, the pupils now rolled back into her skull. The sight of her tongue lolling from her mouth excited him. With a nervous pleasure sweeping over him, he thrust his face forward. To a passing onlooker, it would have appeared he was intending to kiss the dead woman's mouth. But instead, he sunk his teeth into her tongue. Like a dog tussling with a stick, he ripped her tongue free with his teeth and swallowed it whole. His Adam's apple rippled beneath his white skin as the woman's tongue slid down his throat.

Then he placed her head along with her lifeless body in the clearing he had made on the barn floor. He removed his coat and hung it from a nail sticking out from the back of the barn door. Carefully, he unbuttoned the sleeves of his crisp cotton shirt and rolled them to his elbows. Next, smoothing out his leather apron, he knelt beside the woman and set about his work. Using his claws like knives, he cut the woman's clothes into strips. Working his abnormally long fingernails like tweezers, he peeled back the shreds of her dress, exposing the milky-coloured flesh beneath. Her skin was smooth, young, and it opened up like tissue paper, falling from her bones like succulently cooked meat. Once her abdomen was open, he removed her intestines and entrails and placed them on her chest, using it like a platter. Sitting beside her on the floor, he crossed his legs, as if sitting down for a meal. Then he gorged himself on her innards. They felt hot and greasy between his fingers. He ate the liver first, blood and juices running off his chin and splashing his apron. Then her kidneys, lungs, and finally, as if regarding it as dessert, he ate her heart.

His eyes rolled back in their sockets as he savoured every bloody mouthful. When he felt full, he got onto his knees. He took her head and positioned it on the ground at the neck of her body. Then, working with the skill of a surgeon, he removed her eyelids with his fingernails. He wanted her to be able to see what he had done to her for the rest of eternity. He didn't want her to be able to close her eyes on it for one moment.

Still kneeling, he worked his way around her body, and with his tongue, he licked up the streams of blood that had spilt from her. Once satisfied he had licked up every last drop, he stood and licked his fingers clean. The blood was too precious to waste. Returning to the nail in the door, he took his coat, put it on, and fastened the buttons at the front to conceal his apron.

Picking a stringy lump of flesh from between his teeth with his fingernail, his fangs almost seemed to shrink back into his gums, and his claws returned to the shape of finely-manicured fingers. Looking back one last time at the woman on the floor, he licked his lips and then left the barn, disappearing back into the night, as if cloaked by a shroud of fog.

8

I awoke and sat bolt upright, the fragments of a night-mare hazing at the forefront of my mind. I couldn't remember what exactly I had been dreaming about, but my heart was thumping in my chest and I felt scared. I tried to focus on the last fragmented images that swam before me, but to look at them was like trying to stare through a cloud of fog.

I looked around, hoping that perhaps I had awoken on the floor of that train, or better still, my own bed, the last few days a nightmare of their own. I looked to my left and could see a pile of white ash, a spiral of smoke rising from its centre. The blanket that Zoe had given me the night before was wrapped about my shoulders. The sky was clouded over, and a dark, dank cloud lumbered across it. There was a chill breeze and the dry-looking shrubs that surrounded the camp swayed to and fro.

There was a noise behind me, and I looked back over my shoulder to see the preacher cleaning one of his guns with a dirty-looking rag.

"You're awake then," he said, holstering his gun. He was standing next to the wagon, and he reached inside and took hold of a dented-looking tin mug. "Coffee?"

I nodded at him, my mouth tasting like road kill from the elk and chilli beans that I had eaten the night before.

He bent down and handed me the mug. I took a sip and it was lukewarm and tasted very bitter. I grimaced as he stood up, heading back to the wagon. It wasn't Starbucks – but it was coffee and I was grateful for that.

"Where are the others?" I asked him.

Hooking his thumb over his shoulder, he said, "At the river."

Water! I thought. I would have given anything for a nice, warm shower. Running the tip of my tongue over my front teeth, I would have happily given my life for some toothpaste.

Did they have toothpaste in 1888? I doubted it somehow.

I stood up and went back to the rear of wagon. I handed the tin mug back to the preacher and he chucked the remains into the stubby grass that spiked up through the hard-panned ground.

"I don't suppose you have a bath or someplace I could, you know, freshen up?" I asked him.

"Like I said, the river is over there," and he cocked his thumb again back over his shoulder.

"Oh, okay," I nodded.

"Be quick," he said as I headed in the direction he had pointed in. "We have to be in town by noon."

Remembering the meeting that he had planned with the Englishman, I made my way through the shrub which circled the camp. I wondered if this man was connected to me in some way. The preacher had said that we had both arrived here at around the same time. Coincidence? Perhaps. But then again, maybe not. He might know how I could get home.

On the other side of the bushes, I could hear the sound of splashing water and voices. I made my way towards the sounds. I stepped from the undergrowth and found myself on the bank of a fast-flowing river. Harry was standing next to it; four horses were tethered together which were drinking from the water. He looked up at me, nodded, then looked away. Zoe and Louise were further down the riverbank in the opposite direction, and I made my way towards them.

"Hey, Sammy," Zoe said, fixing her dress at the back. Her hair lay in damp-looking tails about her shoulders.

Louise was fastening her gun belt around her waist, and like Zoe, her long black hair lay wet about her shoulders. "Are you okay?" she asked me.

"I just need to have a wash, that's all . . . " I started, and then stopped as my whole question about toothpaste was answered.

Zoe snapped a twig from a nearby bush. Placing it between her front teeth, she gnawed briefly on the end, splitting it into shreds which looked similar to a brush. She then rubbed this back and forward across her teeth as if cleaning them.

"So that's how you do it," I whispered.

"Say what?" Louise asked me with a friendly smile.

"Huh?" I said, looking away from Zoe and at her. "Oh, it's nothing."

"Okay," Louise smiled, snatching up her hat and placing it on her head. Pulling down the brim so I could just about see her brown eyes beneath it, she sauntered away.

"Do you want me to wait for you?" Zoe asked, taking the twig from her mouth and throwing it into the river.

I didn't much fancy stripping off in front of someone I hardly knew, so I casually said, "No, you're okay. I'm just going to have a quick dip and I'll catch you up."

"Are you sure?" Zoe said, watching me.

"Sure," I smiled and turned away.

I waited for the sound of Zoe's boots crunching over the pebbles to disappear, and then looked back. I just caught sight of her, disappearing into the tall shrub. Further down the bank, I could see Harry tending to the horses, and he had his back to me. So as quickly as I could, I pulled off my top, unfastened my guns, and kicked off my boots. I worked my rough-feeling denims down over my hips and as quickly as I could, I ran naked into the stream.

The water was ice-cold, and I gasped. I let it rush over me, dipping my head beneath the fast-flowing current. Even though the water had a numbing effect, it made my skin tingle, making me feel alive again. As I took a cup full of the water in my hands and splashed it across my face and long blond hair, it occurred to me again, that if I were unconscious back in 2012, how had I created a world that seemed so real – so believable? I could feel the ice-cold water streaming down over my breasts, between my shoulder blades, covering my skin in gooseflesh. Would I really be able to create that much detail if I were really caught in some dream? What else would my imagination be able to dream up? What other nightmarish details would I be able to conjure, as I went around and around on that tube train?

Then, as if to prove my mind was able to create anything, I breathed, "Oh shit" and hoped that the giant brown bear which was bounding from the bushes and racing towards the water's edge was a product of my imagination.

9

I looked at the bank and could see my guns winking back at me in the pale sunlight. They were the first things that I thought of – strange, really, as I never owned guns before. Back in London, I would probably have been too scared but to think of anything other than '*Run, Sammy, Run!*'

But this place was different – *I* was different. And my first thought again had been to fight back – to survive. Charging towards the river, the bear reared up on its back legs and roared. It must have stood at least six foot tall, and its whole body seemed to shake at the sound of its own bawling. It swiped at the air, its claws capped with long yellow nails that looked like they would slice my skin from me, as easily as peeling an orange.

The bear dropped onto all fours again and came splashing into the water. I paddled backwards, my legs kicking against the freezing cold current. For a creature so big, it moved quickly through the water towards me. Its dark brown fur glistened, and its giant snout opened to reveal a gum full of razor-sharp teeth. My heart was racing so fast that I could hear it beating in my ears, so loudly it almost drowned out the bear's roars of anger.

Then there was another sound and it boomed like my heart. I looked to my right, water splashing up into my face as the bear raced closer towards me. Harry was running down along the bank towards me, guns held high in his fists. He was firing them over and over again, the sound of them like thunder.

"Hey! Hey!" he was shouting, as if to draw the bear's attention from me and towards him.

"Harry!" I shouted, watching him come racing along the edge of the river, his boots sending up sprays of water.

The bear lunged at me with a giant paw. I ducked beneath the water, some of it spilling into my mouth. I wasn't a great swimmer – not back home anyhow – and being here didn't seem to make much difference. I peered up through the water and could see Harry as he sped along the bank; he appeared to be moving at a great speed – faster than I had ever seen anyone run before. Blinking, I couldn't be sure if watching him through the water was distorting my view – making him appear to be moving faster than he really was – or could.

Needing air, I raised my head above the water and the bear towered over me. It swiped its meaty arms through the air, its claws passing so close to my face that I felt a rush of air spray droplets of water across my cheeks. Then the bear was roaring again, a thick, ropey length of saliva swinging from it jaws. It hit the water just inches from me with its paw, and the splash was so great that I went flying back beneath the water again. A stream of bubbles escaped from my nose and mouth as I gasped for air.

Then, peering up through the water again, desperate to locate the beast, I saw something clinging to its back. It was Harry. Somehow he had managed to launch himself at the bear and now looked to be riding it, like a cowboy rides a wild bull in a rodeo. The bear sliced its claws backwards as it tried to reach for Harry. But he held on tight as the bear shook its body, trying to throw him clear.

Then as the water splashed and rippled above me, I saw Harry pinwheel his arms around in the air so fast, that they became almost a blur. The water suddenly turned red, almost black, as blood sprayed from the bear. Chunks of fur-covered flesh splattered all around me, and even beneath the water; the sound of the bear howling in pain was ear-splitting.

With my lungs feeling like they were going to burst and my head feeling light, I thrust my head above the surface of the water and gulped in large mouthfuls of air. Arming the water from my eyes, I looked up to see Harry still perched on the bear's colossal back. Strips of flesh hung from it in ragged chunks. In one quick flash of movement, Harry drew one of his guns, placed the barrel against the crown of the bear's head and fired. A stream of red mess shot from the bear's open jaws. It buckled beneath Harry, who back-flipped off the bear and landed in the water with a splash.

Like a drunken ballerina, the bear wobbled from side to side, released a rasping groan from the back of its throat, and then collapsed onto its side in the water. I watched as it drifted away from me and downstream. Something snaked its way around my waist and I gasped out loud.

"There's nothing to fear," a voice whispered in my ear.

I glanced over my shoulder to see that it was Harry who had hold of me. With his arm coiled about me, he swam back towards the bank. His arm felt strong, almost crushing the breath from me as he guided me backwards.

"You can let go of me," I wheezed, conscious of the fact I was naked beneath the water.

"Keep calm," he whispered, and I could feel his breath against my ear.

"I'm quite calm, thank you very much," I replied. "Now please let go of me."

"Nearly there," he said, pulling me towards the edge of the water.

Sensing that the river was becoming shallower, I said, "I'm naked."

"I know," he whispered back and pulled me from the water.

He held me against him, and like mine, his body felt as cold as ice.

"You're shivering," he said, his grey eyes concentrating on mine.

"So are you," I replied, looking back into his eyes, which were as grey as stone.

"I'm cold," he whispered, his sandy-coloured hair dripping water onto his face.

"So am I," I told him, wanting to get dressed, but a small part of me enjoying being held by him.

"You don't shiver because you're cold," he said, pressing one of his strong hands into the small of my back, his little finger resting just above the groove of my buttocks.

"Why then?" I asked.

"You shiver because of fear," he said, his lips a grim line across the lower half of his face.

"Fear of what?" I breathed, my breasts pressed flat against his hard, damp chest.

Then that grim-looking line across his face broke

into something close to a smile. "Get dressed," he ordered, "the others are coming." As if dismissing me, he let go and walked away. I hurriedly picked up my clothes at the sound of the others racing towards us through the shrubs. I put on my shirt and denims. All the while, I watched Harry walk away from me back towards the horses. There was something about him I just couldn't figure out. He seemed so distrusting of me last night around the fire, almost angry for some reason. He had made me look like an idiot by giving me whiskey – that hadn't been a mistake. But there was something else, the way he had raced along the shore, how he had suddenly appeared on that bear's back and the wounds he had inflicted on it. Who was Harry Turner? *What* was he? Was he a figment of my imagination? If he was, then perhaps I could get rid of how he had left me feeling – confused, yet excited somehow.

Had I made him feel the same way? I wondered. *Had he enjoyed holding me close to him like that?*

I pulled on my boots and fastened my gun belt, never taking my eyes off him as he walked up the bank. I knew that if he looked back – just once – then he liked me. But he didn't.

Harry might not have looked back, but he was right about one thing, I was scared. Because if Harry was real, along with the others, and I really was in 1888, how was I ever going to get home again?

10

"What happened?" the preacher hissed, running into the clearing, guns drawn. His crystal blue eyes scanned the shore, searching for any immediate threat.

Louise and Zoe appeared close behind him, guns clenched tightly in their fists.

"I was attacked by a bear," I said, flicking my damp hair back from shoulders.

"What bear?" Louise snapped, her guns raised and coat-tails flowing out behind her.

"It's dead now," I said quite calmly.

"You killed it?" Zoe asked me, scanning the shore for its corpse.

"Not me," I said with a shake of my head. "Harry killed it."

"Where is he now?" the preacher asked.

I nodded down the shoreline towards Harry, who was now leading the horses away from the water's edge and back towards camp. The preacher looked back at me.

"Are you okay?"

"Fine," I said back, not knowing if that was really true or not. Half of me just wanted to come clean, to tell the preacher everything. Wasn't he meant to be a man of God, after all? Shouldn't I therefore be able to confide in him – tell him my secrets – and receive his blessings? Maybe if I did tell them I was from the year 2012, unconscious and traveling on a train that snaked its way beneath London, I might disrupt this whole illusion I'd created and they would all just disappear in a puff of smoke. But what if they didn't? I'd be in the crap again, six revolvers aimed at my head.

So grabbing my coat from the ground, I brushed past the preacher and made my way back towards the camp. I heard them slide their guns back into their holsters and make their way after me. Harry had arrived back before us. One of the horses he had reined to the front of the wagon, and the others he had saddled. I watched as he mounted a white horse. It had a long black streak running like a jagged cut down the length of its forehead and muzzle. Although its coat was white, its mane and tail were jet-black. Somehow I knew that it was a Mustang, but I had never seen one with such colouring before. Could I ride, too? As far as I was aware, I had never ridden a horse before – but then again, I had never fired a gun before, but here I was an ace at it.

Zoe and Louise mounted the remaining two horses and the preacher climbed aboard the wagon. From the side I could see that the back wheels were larger than those at the front. I heard Harry make a clucking sound in the back of his throat, and his horse trotted forward. Zoe and Louise followed on theirs.

"Climb up," the preacher said, looking down at me.

Realising that I wasn't going to find out if I could ride a horse or not, I climbed on board the wagon and sat next to the preacher. With one quick flick of the reins, the horse began to move forward. The wagon lurched, and gripping the handrail at the side, I steadied myself.

Reaching for something beside him, the preacher produced my hat, and with a smile barely visible beneath his overgrown moustache, he said, "Don't forget your hat, cowgirl."

I took it from him, and settling back into the wooden seat, I placed it on my head.

PART TWO

Spencer Drake

11

The journey to the town of Black Water Gap wasn't the most comfortable of journeys that I had ever made. The ground was uneven in places and the wagon listed from left to right, and up and down. The horse out front bobbed its head and swished flies and other insects away with its tail. Apart from being uncomfortable and my arse going numb on the wooden seat, we passed across some breathtakingly beautiful country. I had only seen such red-coloured rocks and rugged mountains in picture books before, or in holiday brochures advertising vacations I could never have afforded. To look at the world around me, really, was like looking at all those scenes I had seen in old cowboy films. There really were cactus plants growing out of the ragged ground every few feet, and everything had a dried-out, burnt look to it. Everywhere I glanced, the horizon seemed to be awash with burnt amber colours, yellows and browns. The world looked as if at some time in the ancient past, it had been set alight and left to slowly burn. Although the sun hung high above, that chill wind nagged at me, and I pulled my coat tighter around me.

Harry, Louise, and Zoe rode ahead, their horses trotting next to one another. Every so often they would exchange a few words, but I was too far away to hear what it was they were talking about. I glanced sideways at the preacher, his black hat with the wide brim pulled low over his brow. Apart from his white dog collar, his coat and clothes were all black. Sitting so close to him, I could see that his face was lined with some wrinkles. It was hard to guess his real age. He wasn't unattractive, but he had a look of danger about him. It was his eyes, they were cold and blue, and when he looked at me, it was like he was staring straight into my soul. I thought of the noises he and Louise had made as they'd shagged in the wagon the night before and I wondered if they were really together, or was it just a sex thing? Was a preacher man allowed to take a woman into his bed? I didn't think so, but perhaps things were different back in 1888?

As I sat and studied him from the corner of my eye, he looked at me and said, "What's that tune you whistle?"

"Sorry?" I said, unaware I'd been whistling at all.

"That tune, I've never heard that before."

Then blushing, I realised I'd been whistling the song 'Preacher Man' by Dusty Springfield. I felt like a right idiot. "It's just a song I heard back home, in England," I told him.

"What's it called?" he said, snapping his head to the right and fixing me with his cool stare.

Feeling my cheeks burning, I lied and said, "I can't remember now." How could I confess that I'd been staring at him and whistling that particular song? Not only that, the song hadn't even been written yet and probably wouldn't be for another seventy years or so. I knew I couldn't afford to make another slip-up like that again or I'd be out of time in more ways than one. As I sat and wondered for how long I could keep the pretence up of being brought up in the old west, the preacher asked, "So, you carry guns back in England?"

"Erm . . . " I mumbled.

"It's just that you're a good shot," he said, looking straight at me, as if checking my reaction to his question. "I know many a gunfighter who would sell their own mothers to have the speed and skill that you have."

"Erm . . . " I said again, not knowing what to say. People didn't carry guns in England unless they were a cop or on the wrong side of the law. Like I said, my history wasn't great, but even back in the London of 1888, guns weren't openly carried by people.

"It's just that you've been blessed with a God-given gift or . . . " he started.

"So what faith do you actually preach, *Preacher*?" I cut over him. "Are you a Catholic, Baptist, or something else, because you sure are the strangest holy man that I've ever met."

With his moustache twitching beneath his nose, and his lips pressed together in a thin white line, I wished that I could take back the cocky remark I'd just made. I might have well of just said to him, "Mind your own fucking business," and he knew it. Then, to my surprise, his grimace turned into a smile and he laughed. It was deep and throaty, more like a rasp. He reached inside his coat, and my fingers instinctively hovered over my guns.

The preacher glanced down at my hands, and with that smile still playing on his lips, he pulled out that small wooden box with the smokes from inside his coat. With a flick of his wrist, he opened it and shoved it towards me. With my eyes fixed on his, I took one of the cigarettes and popped it between my lips. Taking one for himself, he put the box away and lit both smokes. I inhaled, my eyes still on his.

"So are you really a preacher?" I asked him, as he blew smoke from beneath his moustache.

"Yep," he said, and looked front.

We travelled in silence for several moments and the urge to tell him everything was overpowering. I wanted to tell him where I was really from, what had happened to me, and how I got here. It was like I wanted to confess; I wanted him to hear my confession.

So, blowing smoke from the corner of my mouth, I looked at him and said, "Preacher, where am I?"

Without looking back at me, he simply said, "Colorado, my dear child, Colorado."

Then the moment was gone, the need to tell him everything had passed. So I said, "What month is it?"

"November," he said, looking at me curiously.

"And the date?"

"Sunday the 11th," he told me, and then added, "Shouldn't you at least know what the date is or is your memory really that shot-through?"

"And if it's a Sunday, shouldn't you be in church or something?" I said right back.

Sensing something was wrong, he rattled the reins, and glancing at me he said, "You have nothing to fear but fear itself, Samantha Carter. You'll find out the reason the Almighty has seen fit to bring you here. There is no such thing as an unanswered prayer."

"I don't ever remember praying for . . . " I started.

"The Lord doesn't always give you what you want," he said, his cold eyes trained on me again. "But he does give you what you need."

"What do I need?" I asked him.

"To know that you were right," he said.

"Right about what?"

"That vampires really do exist," he said, looking front again and whipping the reins. Not another word passed between us until we reached the town of Black Water Gap.

A short distance from the dusty-looking road that cut through the centre of town was a wooden board that had been whitewashed. Written across it in black paint were the words, *Welcome to Black Water Gap*. The wagon trundled past the sign and into town. Men and women passed up and down the streets. Some of these people were dressed better than others. The women, I noticed, wore long, pretty dresses with frills at the ends of each sleeve and at the hems. Others wore dainty gloves and carried lacy umbrellas over their shoulders. Men wore suits, waistcoats with watch chains glinting from them. Their suits were sombre-looking, grey or black in colour. They wore what looked similar to bowler hats on their heads. I had never seen so many men all in one place with long, droopy moustaches. A few children darted along the street, calling out to each other as they chased a wooden hoop. Their feet kicked up plumes of white dust which looked like ash.

I looked in wonder at the buildings, which stood lined on either side of the street. Again, I was struck by how similar everything looked to the movies I had seen. But then I guess, if I were making this whole new world up in my head as I waited to be found in 21st-century London, wouldn't my mind create a reality with images I had previously seen?

We passed a blacksmith's, built from planks of pale wood. The building was tall, with a roof that slanted away on either side. Across the front in black coloured stencil it read, *Smiths – Blacksmith & All Metal Work. Anvil Work – Horse Shoeing – Wagon Workshop*. To my right I saw a small wooden building with the words *Bath House* written across the front of a wooden board that swung to and fro in the wind. Now, I really wouldn't have minded making a stop there. The thought of a nice deep bath full of water to sink into made me miss home more than anything. Next to this there was a telegraph office, but I knew there was no Internet or Wi-Fi here. On the opposite side of the street there was a clean white building, which was raised on a wooden boardwalk, with steps leading up to it. The sign above it read in huge black lettering, *The National Bank*. Now if my mind was creating everything I was seeing, I wouldn't have been too surprised if a group of bandana-covered men burst through the doors in a hail of bullets, clutching bank bags with the '$' sign on the front of them. But we passed it quickly and quietly, there was no gunfire, sticks of dynamite exploding, or bank robbers.

Next to the bank was a larger building, and again, this was raised on a boardwalk. It had wooden pillars supporting a wooden overhang with a sign hanging from it which read, *General Store – Dry Goods and Clothin'*. On the porch there was a stack of barrels and two rocking chairs. In these sat two bearded old men, who played some game on a black-and-red-chequered board.

Ahead I could see Harry, Louise, and Zoe slow their horses outside a tall building. It was on two levels with a railed walkway running around the top of it. Off of this, there were several doors. Fixed to the side of the building, there was a wooden staircase that led up to the walkway and the rooms leading from it. Just like the General Store, there was what looked like a porch leading to a set of thick doors. There were several windows set on both floors and in each of them burnt an oil lamp. The building looked clean and welcoming, and I didn't have to read the sign above the porch to realise it was the town's hotel and saloon.

There was a timber rail fixed to the ground outside, and Harry and the others tethered their horses to it. There was a tin drinking trough, which the horses were quick to bury their muzzles into. The preacher slowed our wagon to a stop and climbed down from the seat, and I followed. The others joined us beside the wagon. Taking a watch and chain from his coat pocket, the preacher looked at it. Then turning to the others, he said, "It's time we met with this Englishman, Spencer Drake."

With his hat pulled low, the long tails of his coat trailing out behind him, the preacher climbed the steps and pushed open the set of batwing doors, and entered the saloon.

12

A wooden bar ran the length of the saloon to the left. There was music, which came from a piano in the corner. The player was stooped over it, seated on a stool. The main floor area was covered in circular tables, and at them sat men who played poker, dominos, and dice. Unlike the westerns I had seen, there wasn't the imposing atmosphere that I had expected. It wasn't like being in a pub in central London, either, but it definitely wasn't like the saloons I had seen in movies. There wasn't any straw on the floor or a string of prostitutes patrolling the wooden balcony that circled the upper floor of the building.

We followed the preacher to the bar and he ordered five beers. To be honest, it was too early in the day for me to start drinking beer, but I wasn't going to say anything. The bitter-tasting coffee which the preacher had given me that morning was the last time I'd drank anything, and my throat had started to feel dry. The bartender was smartly dressed in a clean white apron, and his black hair was greased flat. A circular pair of glasses perched on the bridge of his pointed nose.

He poured the beers from a keg resting on a shelf behind the bar, and the preacher slid a handful of coins across to the bartender, who scooped them up in his fist.

"We're meeting a Mr. Spencer Drake here," the preacher said, then took a sip of the frothy beer. His already-white moustache became covered in the froth and he armed it away.

The bartender eyed him, and then looked along the bar at the rest of us. Turning back to face the preacher, he nodded towards the furthest corner of the saloon and said, "The gentleman you are looking for is seated right over there."

"Bless you," the preacher smiled, tipping the brim of his hat at the bartender. Then, taking his beer, he headed across the saloon. Harry and the others scooped up their drinks and followed him. I took mine, and heading across the room, I took a sip and grimaced. The beer was warm, but it was better than nothing, so I took another sip.

The corner of the room where Spencer Drake waited

for us was the darkest part of the saloon. Even the oil lamps which were fixed to the wall did little to light it. He was seated at a table beneath the stairs that led to the upper balcony. He sat alone with his back to the wall, but even in the semi-darkness, I couldn't help but notice how good-looking he was. His hair was raven black and the ends of it rested against the crisp white collar of his shirt. His skin was fair and smooth-looking, and not one whisker shone through his skin. I glanced over at Harry and the untidy growth that covered the lower half of his face like a dirty shadow. Drake's eyes were of the purest green and they were sharp and piercing. But it was his mouth that I was drawn to. His lips were perfect, with a cupid's bow that any model back home would have died for, and I couldn't help but wonder what it would be like to be kissed by them. Although his face was long and slender, his features were masculine and dominant-looking. Apart from his obvious good looks, which I could see hadn't gone unnoticed by Zoe as she sat with her mouth open like a trap which had been sprung, Spencer Drake was impeccably dressed. Around the collar of his white shirt, he had tied a burgundy-coloured silk tie. He wore a long dress coat, which was charcoal grey with black velvet lapels. Beneath this, he wore a waistcoat, with a gold watch and chain. It wasn't scratched and kept in his coat pocket like the preacher's. His hands were steepled before him and I could see that his fingernails had been clipped perfectly and were clean, not like the rough and dirty hands which Harry had held me with that morning.

Once we were all seated, the preacher spoke. "Spencer Drake?"

"Yes," Drake replied, his voice soft but strong. "And this is your – how should I describe them?" he said, looking at each of us in turn. "Team? Gang? Disciples?"

"There were twelve disciples, Mr. Drake, and they were all men," the preacher corrected him, his cold blue stare an equal match to Drake's piercing green eyes. "It is I who is the disciple, and I follow the path of a man far greater than you or I ever could be."

With a wry smile tugging at the corners of his perfect mouth, Drake said, "I'm sorry; I didn't mean to offend you."

"It's not I you have to fear offending," the preacher said, raising his warm foamy beer and taking a slurp. His eyes didn't leave Drake's once.

"It's just that – how can I put this without offending *anyone*," Drake said. "You don't appear like any holy man that I have ever encountered before."

"The Lord cut his brethren from many types of cloth," the preacher said back, stony-faced.

"But you don't carry a Bible or a crucifix," Drake came back with that half-smile.

"Do I need one, Mr. Drake?" the preacher asked, his eyes now as pale as his skin.

"Which one? A Bible or a cross?" Drake shot back, his voice still calm and even.

"You tell me?" the preacher asked him, a wry smile now tugging at his lips.

"For a man who professes to hunt vampires, I thought one or both would be essential," Drake said.

"And is that why you want to hire us?" the preacher asked him flatly.

"No, not at all," Drake gave a dry laugh. "But before we get down to the true nature of my business with you, let me take a guess at who you all are." Peering out of the gloom at us, he looked at Louise and said, "You must be Louise Pearson." Then, looking at Harry, he said, "Harrison Turner." Switching to Zoe, he said, "Zoe Edgar." Looking at me last, he paused, and then added, "and if I'm not mistaken, you must be Marley Cooper. Why, you are far more beautiful than the rumours would suggest."

"You are wrong," I said, looking back into his eyes. "My name is Samantha Carter and . . . "

"Like me, you are English," he cut in, his eyes seeming to flash momentarily. "Your accent is from London, if I'm not mistaken?"

"Yes," I said.

"And from what part of that great city do you hail from?" he smiled, and that mouth looked so kissable.

"Whitechapel," I told him.

"Whitechapel?" he said, cocking an eyebrow with

interest. "Such an impoverished part of town. And I wager that you are glad you have made good your escape?"

"Escape?" I asked him with a frown, and I could sense that the others gathered around the table were all staring at me.

"Why, such a place as Whitechapel wouldn't be safe for a beautiful young woman such as your good self," he smiled at me again, and I wished he would stop doing that.

"Safe?" I said numbly, my attention drawn back to his mouth.

"Why, the killer of course," he said, his smile fading into a bloodless line. "If you truly have come from Whitechapel, then you surely must have heard of the Ripper? Jack the Ripper?"

"Sure I've heard of him," I said, picking up my glass and taking a sip of the warm beer.

"A terrible, terrible thing indeed," he almost sighed. "Why, only just before leaving London myself, I read in the newspapers of his latest attack. The poor girl's throat had been severed through to her spine, her abdomen had been emptied of organs, and her heart was missing. The papers were full of it."

Somewhere in the back of my mind, a sickening image of a young woman being mutilated crept forward. It was like a dream that I couldn't quite recall. I suddenly felt sick and woozy. Before I truly knew what was happening, a strong hand was gripping my upper arm and pulling me back into my seat.

"Are you okay?" someone asked, and I glanced sideways to see Harry. He had hold of my arm. "You nearly fell into your beer."

"Is she okay?" I heard Spencer ask as he pressed a snow-white hankie into my hand. The skin covering his fingers felt soft like silk.

"It's just the beer," Harry grunted, taking the hankie and handing it back to Drake. "She'll be just fine."

"Maybe it was all the talk of those brutal killings . . . " Drake started as my head began to clear.

"Perhaps," Louise said, looking sideways at me.

"Shall we just get down to business?" the preacher asked, staring into the gloom where Drake almost seemed to shelter.

"Let's," Drake smiled again, as Harry took his seat. "But first, tell me, whatever happened to Marley Cooper? She was one of your *gang* – wasn't she?"

"She's d—," Zoe started, but before she could finish, the preacher had cut over her.

"She doesn't ride with us no more."

"Oh, really?" Drake smiled again, although his eyes didn't. "Why not?"

"It was my fault," Harry said, and we all turned to look at him. "She loved me, but I didn't feel the same way. It became too dangerous for us to work together."

"Dangerous?" Drake said, seizing on the word that Harry had used. "Why dangerous?"

"A girl ain't gonna shoot real straight if she is thinking about cock all day long," Harry said, meeting Drake's curious stare.

There was a pause for silence, and then Drake laughed and said, "I guess not, Turner, I guess not."

With his face as serious-looking as ever, Harry stared across the table at Drake and said, "Now let's talk business."

13

Drake ordered more drinks to be sent from the bar. Once they had arrived, he seemed to sink further into the shadows. Or perhaps it was simply that it was turning dusk outside and there was a little less light coming in through the windows – I couldn't be sure.

The bartender went about the saloon, lighting the oil lamps that were fixed to the walls. The pianist continued to play some kind of honky-tonk music, and the saloon seemed to liven up as the day headed towards night.

"I am a wealthy landowner from the southwest of England," Drake started and took of a sip of whiskey from the glass which he held in is pale hand. "For many generations, my family has mined copper and tin from the land. But sadly, Cornish mining is in decline and many of my kinsmen have emmigrated to more profitable mining districts overseas. As you may already know, many Cornish miners have already started mining in the copper districts of northern Michigan, and have started to spread to many other mining districts. It is rumoured that over ten thousand miners have already departed Cornwall to find work overseas. It is a shame, as Cornwall is such a beautiful and vibrant land," he said. Then looking across the table at the preacher, he added, "Even the Lord himself saw fit to visit my homeland."

As if sensing that he was being tested somehow, the preacher's eyes twinkled as he sat back in his chair and said, "You speak of the legend of Joseph of Arimathea. I know of that fable. It is said that Joseph of Arimathea, who was a tin miner, brought a young Jesus to the Ding Dong mine in the parish of Gulval to speak to the miners. But there is no evidence to support that. It is just a legend – like I said – a mere fable."

A smile tugged at the corners of Drake's mouth and his green eyes almost seemed to gleam at the preacher. "You really are a holy man," he said.

"I've never claimed to be anything else," the preacher said.

I looked sideways at him. Was he really a priest – a preacher? He certainly knew his stuff, but what preacher carried guns, slept with women, and drank hard liquor? If he was a figure I'd created inside my head, then something had gone wrong somewhere. Some wires had gotten crossed.

"So what you're trying to tell us," Louise cut in, "is that you're interested in mining gold here in Colorado?"

"Yes," Drake nodded and that beautiful smile of his faded again. "But not just any mine. I have it on good authority that the Sangre de Cristo Mountains far north of here have mines that are rich in gold and are yet to be truly explored."

The preacher shot a sideways glance at Harry, then stared back at Drake. "And how are you planning on crossing those mountains?"

"With your help," Drake said. "I've heard the rumours about what lives high up there. I have listened to the stories about the nests."

"If they are just stories, why do you need our help?" Harry asked.

"You are vampire hunters, no?" Drake said, and he dabbed at his lips with the hankie that he had earlier offered me.

No one replied; they just sat and stared back at him across the table.

"Okay," Drake smiled, taking the hankie away from his mouth and placing it back in the breast pocket of his suit. "Gunfighters, gunslingers, call yourselves what you want, but I have heard the legends about all of you. How you are responsible for tracking down those that come out from their nests in the mountains and kill." Then, turning his eyes on the preacher, he said, "Or are those stories just fables?"

"Do you know why those mountains are called the Sangre de Cristo Mountains?" the preacher asked him. "Do you know what Sangre de Cristo means?"

His mouth might have been smiling, but his eyes weren't when Drake looked back at the preacher and said, "Blood of Christ, that's what it means, Preacher. It is said to come from the red colour of the mountain at sunrise and sunset. The colour red is said to be even more vivid when those mountain peaks are covered with snow."

"Some say the red is caused by the sun rising and dying each day," the preacher said, his voice now dropping to a harsh whisper, "but others believe that it is real blood that runs over those mountains, like fast-flowing streams."

"And where would the blood come from?" Drake asked, as if trying to stifle a chuckle.

"From the men that the Vrykolakas snatch in the night and feed on," the preacher said, his voice still low, but controlled. "There is a good reason why those mines in the mountains have been left untouched."

"Leave them be," Zoe broke in, her eyes wide. "You will regret waking them from their nests."

Taking his hankie from his pocket again, he pressed it to his beautifully formed mouth, as if hiding a smirk. "Vampires? Nests? Mountains that are awash with the blood of men? Surely, Preacher, just like the story of Jesus and Joseph of Arimathea, it is nothing more than a mere legend."

"I thought you said we were just legends," the preacher breathed, "but you still came looking for us."

Taking the hankie from over his mouth, Drake looked at us, and said, "I will pay you well."

"We don't want your gold," Harry said grimly. "It's no good to the dead."

"Dead?" Drake queried. "You are not dead."

"Not yet," Louise said back. "The journey you consider making is one of suicide. How are you planning to cross the mountains anyhow? On horseback?"

"The Royal Gorge Railroad," Drake said.

"You intend to travel by steam train?" Zoe asked him. "No one is going to let you run a train up into those mountains. They stopped running trains up there when the miners stopped coming back down again."

"I have chartered my own train," Drake told us.

"What train?" the preacher asked him.

"The Scorpion Steam," Drake smiled with a sense of pride. "The fastest steamer there is – nothing will catch us – not even those creatures you claim nest in the mountains."

"And who is going to run it for you?" Louise asked him with suspicion. "Not us."

"No, no, no, my dear Louise Pearson," Drake chuckled again. "I have hired my own crew."

"What crew?" Harry snapped. "You wouldn't find anyone insane enough to take you up there."

Then, reaching into the outer pocket of his suit, Drake

96

removed something and cast his hand across the table. The bright yellow nuggets scattered towards us. They were so bright, they cast a glow across our faces. "Gold," Drake said his voice now serious. "People will do anything for gold."

Zoe made a whistling noise through her teeth as she looked down at it in awe.

"So where do we fit into all of this?" the preacher asked, ignoring the gold that lay before him. "You seem to have everything planned real good already."

Looking out of the shadows in the corner of the room, Drake said, "Now let's just say for argument's sake that your stories about the vampires are true; then wouldn't it make sense for me to have you on board? Wouldn't I benefit from your knowledge of these creatures? Who wouldn't want the help of gunfighters, gunslingers, vampire hunters, or whatever you truly are?"

The preacher glanced at the others, then at me. I looked back. Then, draining the last of his whiskey from his glass, he thumped it down on the table amongst the rocks of gold and said, "When do we leave?"

"Tomorrow night," Drake told him.

The preacher pushed his chair back from the table and stood. "Until tomorrow night then."

"Where are you going?" Drake asked, bemused.

"To make camp for the night," the preacher explained.

"There is no need," Drake smiled again. "I have taken the liberty of booking you each a room here tonight."

A bed! A real bed! I screamed inside. I really could have kissed Drake now.

"That was rather presumptuous of you," Louise said, looking at him. "How did you know that we would accept your offer?"

Pushing the gold towards her with one long hand, he winked at her and said, "Gold, Louise Pearson. Gold!"

But as we each got up from the table, leaving Spencer Drake to the shadows, I knew the preacher wasn't going up into those mountains in search of gold – he was looking for something else altogether.

14

My room was far better than I imagined it to be – but hey, if I was creating all this stuff up in my head – then why not give myself some luxury? There was a bed, and diving onto it like a kid at a slumber party, I was surprised by its softness. The floor was covered in a thick rug, and I yanked off my boots so I could feel it beneath my tired feet. Beside the bed, there was an oil lamp with a glass shade. The lamp had already been lit for me. There was an open doorway leading off from my room, so I took a peek inside. To my amazement, it was a bathroom. There was no toilet, but a china bowl on the floor with a covering over it. But there was toilet paper! And more than that, there was a tin tub in the centre of the small room and someone had filled it with hot water.

Pulling off my clothes, I sunk beneath the water. The tub wasn't long enough for me to stretch out fully. I had to draw my knees up slightly, but it was better than the river with the grizzly bear. With my shoulders beneath the water, I rested my head back against the rim of the tub and thought of how Harry had rescued me. I closed my eyes and tried to remember him running along the riverbank. He seemed to have moved very fast, but had that been the water distorting my view of him? But the bear – Harry had almost torn it to shreds. The water had turned almost black with blood. But these people were different than those back home – back in the London of 2012. We didn't really have to fend for ourselves. We could have anything and everything whenever we wanted it. We were spoilt. We didn't have to face down bears while taking a wash. The preacher and the others were rougher – hardened – they lived in a world where they had to survive from day to day.

And what of Spencer Drake? He was definitely good-looking, and I suspected he knew it. Whereas his looks were more refined–gentlemanly, Harry was rougher looking – but hot. It was a shame that both came across as being arrogant jerks. Why had I gone and created two hot guys, but given them both zero personality?

With the water starting to turn cold, I reached for a towel that hung from the wall, and climbed from the tub. Wrapping the towel about me, I headed back into the bedroom. It was then I noticed that one of the windows was open and the curtain flapped slowly in a cold breeze. Shivering, I crossed the room to shut the window. Looking out I saw the preacher and the others standing in the street below. The preacher was unfastening the horse which had drawn the wagon. He then went to the rear of the vehicle and reappeared, holding a saddle in his hands. I watched him saddle up the horse then mount it. The others followed. It was then I realised that they were leaving; but why weren't they taking me with them? With a sense of panic rising inside of me, I pushed open the window and shouted, "Hey, Preacher, where are you going?"

Without so much as a glance back at me, the four of them raced out of town. I dropped the towel and pulled on my clothes and gun belt. Perhaps they had told Spencer Drake why they were leaving. I left my room, rushed along the upper balcony, down the wooden stairs, and back into the saloon. I headed through the throng of drinkers who sat at the tables and into the corner. The table where Drake had sat was now deserted; he had gone just like the others. I headed back towards the bar, and drawing the bartender's attention, I said, "The people that I arrived with earlier, did they leave a message for me?"

The bartender shook his head without looking up from the glasses that he was wiping with a cloth. "No message," he said.

"Have they booked out?" I asked him. "Are they coming back?"

The bartender put aside the glass and took a leather-bound ledger from beneath the bar. He thumbed through it. Looking over the rim of his spectacles at me, he said, "No they haven't checked out. I guess they'll be back from wherever it is they've gone."

Feeling a slight sense of relief, I left the bar and headed back out into the night. I descended the steps that led down to street level. It was cold, and it didn't take long for my nose and ears to turn numb. The main street was almost deserted; the only sound was of people coming from the saloon behind me as they laughed and sung along to the honky-tonk music which continued to be played. I looked at the wagon, and guessed that the preacher and the others would be back. But where had they gone? What sort of cowgirl was I going to be if I couldn't even control the characters that I had created inside my head? I looked up at the night sky and there seemed to be less stars out tonight, hidden by a swath of cloud that streaked across the sky. I had been here three days, I guessed. But how long had I been missing from home? If I wasn't lying on the floor of that tube train waiting to be discovered, and I really had been snatched back in time, had anyone noticed that I had gone missing yet? Both my mother and father were dead. They died within a year of each other, two years ago. They had me fairly late in life, but that had never stopped them giving me a great childhood. In fact, I had been spoilt by both of them, particularly my father. But my mum had gotten cancer. It ravished her – ate her up – in the space of a few short months. She went from being a rather buxom woman to a mere skeleton. To watch her fade away like that had been agony; but nothing compared to the pain I felt watching my dad pine for her once she had left us. He had also been active in his retirement, but once on his own, it was like he gave up. He couldn't live without my mum. Then, on the anniversary of her death, he went to bed and never woke up. The post-mortem report stated that he had been in good health – but I knew he had died of a broken heart; but how do you record that on a form?

But there was Sally. Had she noticed I hadn't come home? Or had she been on some three day shag-a-thon, shacked up in her room, enjoying the pleasures of her latest fling? I could remember her being locked away in her room for six days once. What they both did for food and water I will never know, but the noises that had come from her room were incredible. I remember Karl and me trying to make a few of our own, to drown out Sally's – but Karl only ever brought me to a mere whimper that usually sneaked from between my lips, five minutes after climbing into bed together.

Why did Sally always have the fun? And I knew that if it was left to her, my missing person's report wouldn't be filed for a few days yet. What about Karl – it was over between us – he had moved on. So who was going to miss me?

I pulled my coat about me and headed down Main Street, wondering what else my subconscious mind would make up. The street was lined with tall posts that had flames burning atop of them. The flames licked back and forth in the wind which had started to pick up. I passed a white-washed building that had *U.S. Marshal's Office* written across the front. Lamps burnt warmly from within, and with my head bent low, I passed on the other side of the street. I wasn't afraid of the law, I had done nothing wrong as far as I knew, but I didn't want to draw attention to myself by the local law enforcers. Next to the Marshal's office, there was a courthouse. Of all the buildings in the town, this one looked the biggest and cleanest. Just like the Marshal's Office, it was made of wood and painted pristine white. It had a triangle overhang which was supported by four large, white pillars. Then at the end of the street, I saw a church with a steeple that stretched up into the night sky. Moving closer towards it, I could see that it was more of a chapel than a church. I walked up to its front door and turned the handle. Why I wanted to go inside, I didn't know. The last time I had set foot inside a church had been for my father's funeral, and I took that opportunity to snatch several bottles of holy water. Maybe I was hoping to find another holy man other than the preacher. I wanted to see if he was anything like the so-called holy man who was going to lead me up into the mountains. The chapel door swung open, and I stepped inside. The smell of candle wax was almost intoxicating, as was the atmosphere that the flickering candlelight created. The church was empty, and as the door slowly shut behind me, drowning out the sound of the revellers in the saloon, it was like I had fallen into a well of silence.

There were several rows of benches that all faced a huge wooden cross which was suspended from the wall before me. I passed amongst the pews and sat on one end. I could never really remember praying before, only as a kid before bedtime. Looking up at the cross, I said, "If this really is just a dream, let me wake up. Let me go home."

The wind whistled around the eves outside, almost as if in answer to my prayer. What the answer was, I didn't know. Then looking down, I saw a small, silver cross winking back at me from the floor. It was a set of rosary beads. I picked them up and they felt cold in the palm of my hand. I tucked them into my trouser pocket. Standing up, I headed back towards the rear of the chapel. Missed as I had entered, I now saw a small table set against the wall. It was covered with a thin, white lace and several small bottles. In neat black hand-writing, someone had written *Holy Water* across each one. Taking one of the bottles, I placed it into my coat pocket. I remember reading somewhere back home that guns meant didly-shit against vampires – crucifixes and holy water was what counted. As I slipped out of the chapel and back into the night, I realised that all I needed now was a pocketful of garlic and I'd be armed just like I had been back on that tube train.

While I'd been in the chapel, the clouds had dispersed and a full moon hung in the sky. It looked huge, with a hazy blue tinge around it. The moon had never looked as big or clear as when I had looked up at it hanging in the night sky back home. Whistling the song 'Blue Moon' by The Marcels to myself, I made my way back up Main Street, wondering if the preacher and the others had returned. As I made my way along the dusty street, I noticed a small structure nestled between two bigger buildings. The exterior had been painted a dark brown and the door and window frames had been painted green. The sign hanging above the door read *Newspaper Office*. To the left of the door stood a stack of what looked like old newspapers. With the wind picking up, one of the newspapers fluttered from the top of the pile and scuttled towards me. I bent down and snatched it up before it had a chance to get away from me. Wondering what was breaking news in this part of the world in 1888, I turned the paper over in my hands, then gasped. Splashed across the front in bold black letters was the headline:

Local Woman Found Mutilated

With moonlight streaming over my shoulder, I read the article which gave a horrific account of the murder of a woman from the neighbouring town of Crows Ranch. She had been found the previous day by the shoesmith as he had arrived for work. The victim had been beheaded and her innards removed. Letting the newspaper slip from my fingers and flutter away along the street, I could at once see the similarities to the murders being committed by Jack the Ripper in London of 1888 and the London of 2012.

With my hands thrust into my coat pockets to protect them from the cold, I made my way back to the saloon and up to my room. I couldn't help but wonder if the murders were connected somehow. Had the murders all been committed by the same killer? That would be impossible, right? Not only had the murders taken place over five thousand miles apart, they had also taken place with a one-hundred-and-twenty-four-year gap between them.

Once in my room, I took off my coat and lit one of the hand-rolled cigarettes the preacher had given me. With streams of blue smoke jetting from my nose, I sat on the end of my bed and tried to make some sense of the killings. Could they really have been committed by the same killer? Or had the police been right – the murders committed in 2012 had been the work of the copycat Jack the Ripper? But one thing that I wouldn't budge on – one thing that I wouldn't change my mind about – was that I still firmly believed that the killings in 2012 were the work of a vampire.

The saloon had emptied for the night. It was now quiet in the town of Black Water Gap, and as I sat in my room and tried to figure out where I was and why I was here, I heard the sound of a horse trotting down Main Street. I turned down my lamp and went to the window. Hidden behind the hem of the curtain, I watched Louise approach the saloon. She was on her own. The horse stopped, and in the light of the moon, I spied on Louise as she dismounted and tethered the horse to the wooden rail. Then, looking over her shoulder to make sure she wasn't being watched, she crossed over to the horses' drinking trough. Then raising her hands, she quickly plunged them into the water and washed away the blood that covered them in long crimson streaks.

Then, as if somehow sensing that she was being watched, Louise suddenly looked up at me. I quickly stepped away from the window, and slipped back into the shadows, praying that I hadn't been seen.

15

Her eyes were dark like chocolate, her skin was pale, and her light brown hair had started to grey in little wispy tufts around her ears. Like her eyes and hair, her dress was brown and he slowly undid the buttons that ran down the front of it. Beneath her dress he found a petticoat, and this annoyed him – just another layer to remove before he got to what he had come for. He removed her flannel knickers and black woollen stockings. He had already disregarded her boots and straw bonnet.

Before slitting her throat, they had been intimate; but only briefly. He hadn't been interested in her for that; the sex part never really interested him. He wanted something else altogether. The thirst was bad tonight, like he had swallowed a red-hot poker. He knew her blood would soothe the fire that raged in his throat and out across his chest like fingers coated with lava.

Taking her clothes, he folded them into a neat pile and placed them against the wall of the outhouse. It was dark, but he could see clearly – he could see everything. The dark was good. He liked the way it seemed to wrap itself around him like another layer of skin. With his legs crossed, he sat beside the woman and looked at her naked corpse. He touched her breasts with the tips of his long, white, bony claws, and shuddered at the warmth that still radiated from her. She had yet to turn cold. Taking one of her hands in his, he raised it to his mouth. He traced the tip of her forefinger over his lips and sighed deeply. The smell of her skin was wonderful – intoxicating. It made that feeling of burning within him seethe all the more fiercely. Although it was agony, it somehow brought him pleasure and he wanted to make it last for as long as he could, because he knew once he started, it would be over all too soon.

Unable to resist any longer, he sliced through the soft tissue of her finger with his fangs, then through the knuckle, as easily as if it were made of matchwood. The crunching noise coming from his jaws sounded as if he were chewing on broken glass. The skin and bone were just waste to him, it was the blood he wanted, and he sucked on the end of her finger like a straw. The blood gushed into his mouth, and he gulped it down, *that burning feeling in his throat and chest fading away. But not fast enough.*

Using his claws, he drew one of his hooked nails down the length of her body from her breastplate to her pelvic bone. Peeling her open, he removed her intestines, placing them on the dusty floor just above her right shoulder. The entrails glistened like a nest of oily snakes. His hands were hot and sticky with blood and he licked them clean – slowly, his white eyes rolling all the way back into his skull.

Then, tightening his apron, he set about gorging himself until he could eat no more.

16

I woke with a start. Sweat covered me and I looked about the room, not knowing who or where I was. Sunlight poured through a narrow gap in the curtains hanging at the window. I held the rough, woven blanket which covered me about my shoulders and climbed out of bed. At the window, I peeled back the curtains and peered out, and then I remembered. Seeing the dusty main street below, with its wooden buildings and horses, soon reminded me I was in 1888. When was I going to wake back up in 2012? When would I discover why I was here – that's if I really was?

Tethered to the rail below stood the preacher's horse, along with the others'. They must have come back during the night. I remembered spying on Louise as she had made her return alone, washing the blood from her hands in the drinking trough. She had looked up, but had she seen me?

I went to the bathroom, peed, washed, and got dressed. I fixed the gun belt about my waist. There was a mirror attached to the wall beside the bed and I looked at my reflection. What the fuck was I doing? Why was I dressed as a cowgirl? Why was I carrying guns and a belt full of bullets? This wasn't me – this wasn't the Samantha Carter who had grown up in London, studied criminology, who had had two loving parents who had died within a year of each other. The person looking back at me wasn't the Sammy who had shared a flat with a beautiful-looking nymphomaniac and had recently broken up with a guy called Karl. To look at my own reflection was like looking into the eyes of a stranger. The only thing that we both had in common was that we both believed in the existence of vampires.

I closed the bedroom door behind me and passed along the balcony. At the foot of the staircase, I made my way into the saloon, which was empty, apart from Louise who sat at a table on her own. She glanced up. Had she seen me spying on her last night? I worried. But so what if she had? I hadn't done anything wrong. It hadn't been me washing blood from my hands in the middle of the night. She looked up at me and smiled, so I crossed the room towards her.

"Morning," she said, pouring me a mug of coffee from a pitcher that was on the table.

The coffee smelt strong and wonderful and I took in a mouthful. It wasn't as bitter as the stuff the preacher had concocted by the campfire. Set before Louise on the table was a plate, which I guessed had earlier contained her breakfast.

"Do you want to eat?" she asked me.

"Sure," I said. Then not knowing exactly what was on the menu, I added, "What do they have?"

"The eggs are good," she said, pouring herself a mug of coffee from the pitcher. It was then I noticed a piece of blood-stained cloth wrapped about her right wrist. She saw me staring at it. Then, looking over my shoulder at the bartender, she said, "Could we have another plate of eggs over here?"

I sipped from the mug and the black coffee tasted wonderful as I peered down at Louise's bandaged wrist.

"I cut myself last night," she said, placing her hand beneath the table and out of sight.

"How did you do that?" I asked, trying to sound concerned more than curious.

"I tripped," she said, staring at me.

"Is that when you and the others rode off?" I said, looking at her over the rim of my mug.

"Sure," she smiled back.

There was a moment's uncomfortable silence, so I said half-jokingly, "I thought you had left town without me."

"And why would we do that?" she asked me.

114

"Dunno," I shrugged, still staring at her.

"You're one of us now," she smiled.

"Am I?" I said, not knowing if I should be happy about that fact.

"The preacher says so."

The bartender arrived with my plate of eggs. There were three and they looked soft and runny. Not how I liked them, but I was hungry. Beside the eggs sat what looked like a mound of pink mashed potato. I couldn't show my lack of knowledge by asking Louise what the pile of pink stuff was, so I poked at it with my fork and took a small bite. By the taste I guessed it was beans which had been mushed into a pulp, then had been seasoned with onion, salt, and pepper. To be honest it tasted good, so I forked some more into my mouth.

"So what does that mean, exactly?" I asked Louise around a mouthful of the pink stuff.

"What's that?" she asked me, taking a sip of coffee.

"You said that I was one of you now," I reminded her.

"You get to tag along," she smiled.

"To where?"

"Up into the mountains," she said right back.

"And what if I don't want to tag along with you and the preacher?" I said, cutting one of the fried eggs in half.

"Got a better offer?" she asked.

I chewed the egg and looked at her. She was real pretty and I wondered why she *tagged* along.

"So where did you all go off to last night?" I asked her. "If I'm tagging along, how come you didn't take me with you?"

"The preacher had some business he had to settle before we leave for the mountains tonight," she explained. "That's all."

"What sort of business?" I pushed gently, not wanting to sound as if I were interrogating her in any way.

"Just business," she smiled and took in another mouthful of coffee.

Knowing that she was politely telling me to mind my own business, I asked, "They're back now, right?"

She nodded.

"Are they joining us for breakfast?" I asked, trying to sound as casual as I could.

"No, we won't be seeing them until tonight," she said.

"How come?" I asked, sensing that I was pushing my luck now, but needing to know.

"They had a long night and they didn't arrive back until just before dawn, so they are going to rest today," she smiled, her eyes twinkling. "If I were you, I'd do the same. We have a long journey ahead of us."

I didn't know if I'd get away with asking her any more questions about what the preacher and the others had gotten up to overnight, so I tried to change the subject.

"Are you and the preacher together?" I asked her outright.

"Together?" she cocked an eyebrow at me.

Now that I had started down this line of conversation, I knew I couldn't go in reverse.

"It's just . . . the other night I heard you and the . . . " I flushed.

"I'm sorry about that," and Louise's cheeks turned as pink as mine. We both laughed and I felt as if the last few minutes of mutual distrust had melted away. "It's just that the preacher can be . . . how can I put it? A bit wild at times. A real animal."

Remembering the noises that I'd heard coming from the wagon, I smiled and said, "I didn't know preachers were allowed to . . . you know . . . "

"Fuck?" she cut in, her eyes twinkling.

"Well, yeah," I whispered, looking back over my shoulder to see if anyone had overheard her.

"This one does," she smiled wistfully.

"Is he . . . " I started.

"He's the best," she said, before I'd the chance to finish.

With my cheeks burning and my breakfast forgotten, I said, "What I was going to ask was, is he like, a real preacher?"

"He was," Louise said. "Once – but that was a long time ago."

"What happened?" I asked her.

"He lost his faith," Louise said, and her voice sounded kind of sad about that.

"How come?"

"That's his story to tell, not mine," she said, looking at me. And again she looked sad – no, haunted.

Picking up my mug again, I said, "Do you love him?"

Then, fixing me with her pretty eyes, she said, "You don't fall in love with men like the preacher."

"Why not?" I asked her.

"Because they will just introduce you to a world of pain," she said wistfully.

"And what about Harry?" I said.

Then, as if studying me for a moment, she whispered, "Do yourself a favour, Sammy, keep away from Harry Turner."

"Why?" I asked, my interest now suddenly alive.

"Harry is dangerous," Louise said, pushing her chair back from the table and standing up as if to leave.

I looked up at her and said, "How dangerous?"

"There is only one person who could really know how to explain how dangerous Turner is – but Marley Cooper isn't here anymore." Then she was gone, heading back across the saloon.

I swivelled around in my seat, and as she reached the bottom of the stairs leading up to the balcony, I called out, "Who was Marley Cooper?"

Ignoring my question, Louise paused, looked back at me and said, "We leave at dusk. Be ready." Then she was heading up the stairs, and I watched her disappear into the preacher's room and close the door.

I sat at the table and looked down at the half-eaten eggs and pink mush. Apart from being trapped in 1888, things weren't right. Everything was wrong. But what did I do? Did I go along with Louise and the others on this trip up into the mountains where vampires were believed to nest, or did I go . . . go where? I knew no one in 1888, apart from this ragtag group of misfits I had accidently fallen in with. But had it been an accident? There had to be a reason, right? Did the preacher and his gang hold the answers to my questions? Did they hold the key that would get me home?

17

I tried to sleep – but I really couldn't. I lay on the bed
in my room and shifted from my side, onto my back,
front, then onto my side again. It was like one of those
nights when thoughts get stuck in the middle of your
mind that you just can't shake free. I didn't just have
one thought, I had many going around and around
inside my head, and each just led to another thought,
then another question, to the point where I actually
started to wonder if I hadn't gone mad.

I closed my eyes, squeezed them shut so tight that
tears streamed down my cheeks. With my eyes closed,
I tried to picture myself lying back in my bedroom in
2012. I tried to conjure the smells of fresh clean linen,
the sounds of cars passing outside, Sally and her latest
fling getting it on in the room next door. I hoped that

if I really pictured it, got an essence of home in my mind's eye, then I would wake up back in my room and this would have all been a dream.

Slowly I would open my eyes, my long lashes like a spidery haze before me, and take a look around – but each time, I found myself back in that room above the saloon. The oil lamps attached to the walls, the sounds of horses trotting past outside, and the honky-tonk music seeping up from below.

Maybe the answer to me getting home lay in the man who had gripped me from behind on the train – after all, it was him who I had last been with before waking up here. So closing my eyes again, I tried to imagine the choking – suffocating – sensation of his arm tight about my throat. I pretended I could smell his musty coat and feel the coldness of his breath against my cheek. Then, with my eyes screwed tight, I tried to remember the sound of his voice and what he had said to me before that bright white light had flooded the train.

Why are you following me? He had breathed in my ear.

I could hear his voice in my head as if he were lying behind me.

I know what you are, I whispered inside my head.

And what is that? He whispered back.

"You're a vampire," I said, but this time not inside my head, but out loud. I imagined his arm tightening about my throat and I squeezed my eyes shut tighter still.

In my mind I struggled against him, trying to twist my neck to the right so I could see his face. Then I felt him – as if I was back on that train – running one long, bony finger down the length of my cheek.

Oh, Sammy, you don't remember, he said softly inside my head.

"How do you know my name?" I asked aloud, taking the holy water from my coat pocket just like I had before.

How quickly you have forgotten, he teased, and I remembered his breath, stale and old.

I pictured the carriage lights flickering out, and I threw the holy water over my shoulder. I heard him chuckle softly, and the lights came back on inside my head.

Sammy, you really have forgotten, haven't you? he said, and it seemed so real, that he could have been behind me.

Holy water doesn't work, nor does the garlic I can smell in your pocket, or the crucifix which glistens between your breasts, he teased, and I touched the cross which hung around my neck.

"What have I forgotten?" I cried, his grip feeling so real that it was almost suffocating.

"That we've got a train to catch," he said.

But something was wrong, that's not what he said

back on that train. Then I felt him grip my arm and shake me.

"That's not what you said," I shouted, my eyes still closed tight shut.

Maybe this was it? I had done it – I was back on the underground train in London 2012. That's why what he was saying to me had changed. I was beginning to wake – the whole 1888 trip had been something my mind had created as I'd slipped into unconsciousness as he strangled me.

"Wake up!" he said.

"Yes! I want to wake up!" I whispered. "I want that more than anything." Then, opening my eyes, expecting to find myself looking down the length of the train carriage as we rattled into Liverpool Street Station, I found myself looking into the eyes of Harry Turner.

"What are you doing in here?" I asked him.

"Don't flatter yourself, I've come to wake you, that's all," Harry said staring down at me.

"But we're on a train," I muttered, feeling groggy and confused.

"Not yet, girl, but if you don't get your shit together, then we're gonna miss one," he said gruffly, taking my coat off a nearby chair and throwing it at me.

I rubbed my eyes with the backs of my hands, and looking around I could see I was still in my room back in 1888.

"But I was on a train and this was all a dream . . ."

I started, realising that I must have fallen asleep after all.

With his mouth turned down, and fixing me with his grey eyes as I stared vacantly up at him, he shook his head and said, "If your brains were dynamite, there wouldn't be enough to blow your own nose with. Now c'mon."

Then he was gone, the sound of his boots echoing as he headed away along the balcony outside my room.

With my grogginess beginning to clear, and understanding the insult he had just paid me, I shouted after him, "I'm not stupid, you know! I just need to figure out what I'm doing in this godforsaken place."

But just as Harry hadn't looked back at me down at the riverbank, he didn't say anything back this time, either.

"Arrogant jerk!" I hissed under my breath, and made my way after him.

18

The others were gathered outside by the horses. Even though the sun was fading fast, I couldn't help but notice that the preacher looked tired and drawn. At first I wondered if Louise and he hadn't been training for the Sex Olympics again, but I could tell it was more than that. His usually bright, piercing eyes seemed faded somehow – like a washed-out blue. The preacher's face looked drawn and wan, and the wrinkles around his eyes cut deep grooves down both sides of his face and over his temples.

I looked at Zoe, and her usually smooth, youthful skin was so pale, she looked as if she might just faint at any moment. Her blond hair looked almost colourless, like wisps of finely cut tracing paper poking out from beneath her wide-brimmed hat. She caught me looking at her, and instead of flashing me a bright, cheery smile like I had come to expect from her, she just nodded her head at me, and pulled the rim of her hat down low over her eyes. Then glancing over at Harry in the fading light, I could see that he, too, looked paler than usual. But unlike the preacher and Louise, his grey eyes looked just as keen and sharp as they had in my room minutes before.

"Are you guys okay?" I asked them.

"Fine," Louise said, mounting her horse, even though I hadn't asked her. Louise looked sassy as ever in her long dark coat, denims, and boots. Her guns winked back flashes of the dying sun as she straddled her horse.

I watched the preacher and Zoe mount their horses, and the preacher sat forward in his saddle as if he was going to fall asleep at any moment. "What about the wagon?" I asked, noticing it was no longer outside the saloon.

"We won't need that where we're going," the preacher said without looking at me. Dust blew along the main street, and like the others, he pulled the brim of his hat so low over his face, it almost touched the tip of his nose. "Besides, I traded it for another horse," he said in a hushed tone.

"Another horse?" I asked.

"You can ride, can't you?" Harry said, staring at me.

Now, I didn't know if I could or not. I think the closest I'd ever come to riding a horse was as a kid, when my mum and dad took me on holiday one summer to Brighton. They paid for me to ride a donkey along the shore. Was that the same thing? I didn't think so. But then again, I had never fired a gun or fought with five men before – but here I had. In this place, I was like something close to Jason Bourne on crack – but why?

Harry led a huge white horse towards me by its reins. The horse raised its head up and down, then calmed. I wasn't afraid of the horse. Harry looked into my eyes, and I took the reins from him. Not really knowing if I was doing the right thing or not, I just followed my instincts, like I had when drawing my guns. I gently patted the horse's muzzle, then gripping the saddle and placing one foot into the stirrup, I hoisted myself up. I could still feel Harry's eyes on me, so straightening my back, and keeping my elbows loose, I gently squeezed the sides of the horse with my calves and it slowly moved forward. I let my arms and shoulders relax. I pulled gently on the reins and the horse stopped.

"What's its name?" I asked, looking down at Harry.

"Moon," Harry said, trying to mask a look of surprise. Part of me suspected he hadn't believed I could ride. The other half of me suspected that I couldn't ride, either. But I could, and I didn't know how. Just like I didn't know how I could draw my guns so quickly, or how I could disarm five men and kill them all without even raising my heartbeat.

I looked away from Harry as the preacher clucked at his horse and slowly rode away from the front of the saloon. Louise and Zoe followed and so did I. Within moments, Harry had passed me on his horse and was riding alongside the others.

I rocked back and forth in time with Moon, remembering to keep my back straight and elbows relaxed. Had someone taught me to ride at some point? I couldn't remember. When would that have taken place – at some time in my future, or in a past which I couldn't recall?

The ride to the train station didn't take long. It stood just on the outskirts of town. There was only the one platform and a small waiting room and ticket office. Both had been constructed out of the same sun-bleached wood as the buildings back in town. Above the front of the doors, a sign had been fixed and it read, *Black Water Gap Railroad Station*. There were no other passengers that I could see.

"Whoa," the preacher breathed, pulling gently back on the reins. His horse stopped with a nod of its head. During the short distance that we had travelled, the sun had almost faded away on the horizon, leaving behind a pink hazy strip of light. The sky had started to grow dark, and with it I noticed the preacher, Harry, and Zoe had started to look more like themselves. The preacher swung down out of his saddle, the tiredness, which had seemed so crippling before, now gone. We all dismounted and approached the front of the station.

Slowly, the double doors swung open and Spencer Drake stepped from the shadows that seemed to lurk inside.

As he stood before us, a wooden walking stick in his hand, I realised for the first time how tall the man was. He stood over six-foot-three and his frame was slender. His black hair was swept off his forehead, and his green eyes shone like cat's eyes in the twilight. He smiled and I was reminded of how perfect his mouth was. He walked towards us, lifting his walking stick and carrying it over his shoulder. He didn't appear to limp or have any disability, so I guessed the walking stick was some kind of bling more than anything else. He was dressed in a grey suit, waistcoat, and black boots, which gleamed with polish. As he stood before us in his dark clothes and pale face, I couldn't help but think that he looked like a magician's wand.

"Good evening, Preacher," he said, then nodded quickly at the rest of us, as if acknowledging our presence. "Are you ready?"

"Ready for what?" Harry grunted, although Drake hadn't been addressing him.

With a smile tugging at the corner of his lips, Drake eyed Harry and said, "Anything, I guess."

Stepping away from his horse, the preacher approached Drake and said, "That might be closer to the truth than you believe."

"I believe in a lot of things, Preacher," Drake said

back, "but not in myths and legends – just the things that I can see and touch."

"A skeptic?" Zoe cut in, eyeing Drake up and down.

"Just like Thomas the Disciple," the preacher smiled at Drake. "He didn't believe that the Lord had been resurrected until he saw Jesus's wounds."

"What are you saying?" Drake smiled back at the preacher, "That I too need to see wounds of some kind before I will believe in these vampires that you talk of?"

"Blessed are they who have not seen, and yet have believed," the preacher said.

"Is that what you say?" Drake asked him.

"No, that's what the good Lord says," the preacher winked back at him with a grim smile.

There was a silence as Drake stared back at the preacher. Then, the silence was broken by the sound of the station doors swinging open. This was followed by the noise of metal being drawn against leather and I looked around to see the preacher and the others had all drawn their guns at the sight of a man who was stepping clear of the waiting room. I looked down at my hands, and could see that I too had drawn my own guns.

Raising his free hand before him, Drake said, "There is no need for alarm." Then, gesturing the stranger forward from the shadows, he added, "Let me introduce you to my physician, Marcus Dable."

130

"What do you need a doctor for?" the preacher breathed, slowly lowering his guns. "Are you sick?"

Drake waited for us all to holster our guns before he spoke again. "I have anemia."

"What's that?" Zoe asked him.

"A blood disorder," he said gravely. "My blood does not carry enough oxygen to the rest of my body. It can often leave me feeling weak and tired." Then taking the walking stick from where he had it rested over his shoulder, he added, "Sometimes I can feel so tired and weak that I need a stick to keep me upright. Do not be alarmed by the presence of my doctor. He is here to assist me, to keep me in good health."

"Great," Harry sighed. "It's bad enough we're even venturing up into those mountains, let alone taking along someone who hasn't got the faintest idea what they are heading into, and now admits that's he going to be as fast in a fight as a crippled turtle."

"I'm not a cripple," Drake said flatly. "Do not concern yourself with my health, Turner. I pay my doctor to do that."

"My employer is quite right," Dable suddenly spoke up. "I will do my very best to keep him in good health over what you suggest could be a very hazardous journey. He will not hinder you in any way."

"He better not," Harry said. "Because if we start getting crapped on from a great height, I ain't providing him with no umbrella."

"You should have told us you had a disease," the preacher said.

"Why, would you have turned me away?" Drake asked him with a raised eyebrow.

The preacher stared back at Drake as if considering his reply, but then slowly looked into the distance and said, "I believe this is our train."

All of us followed the preacher's stare, and out of the distance, I could see a column of black smoke belching up into the darkening sky. The whole ground seemed to rumble and shake as the steam train roared towards us like a giant black scorpion. Steam hissed and spat from around the pistons that drove the wheels. The driver blew up on his horn, the sound tearing the approaching night in half with its smoking roar. The train slowed as it neared the station, and thick clouds of dirty smoke wafted around us. It was choking and smelt acrid. I covered my nose with my hand and pulled my hat low over my eyes as they began to water.

"Isn't she beautiful," Drake said, more as a statement of fact rather than a question, leading us around the outside of the waiting room and onto the platform. The train was definitely a monster. A huge, pointed cow catcher jutted from the front of the engine like an iron pincer. The engine itself was long and sleek with one giant black funnel, which continued to fill the night with plumes of black smoke. It was like a dragon was living inside of its metal body. The cab was painted black as was the tender, which was overflowing with coal, and along its side in silver writing were the words *Scorpion Steam*. Although the train was like some ancient beast, it was sleek-looking, with the silver rings that circled the funnel, and a silver headlight at its front. In fact, as I looked along the length of the train, different parts shimmered brightly in the dark. The carriage door handles were all silver, as were the window frames, and the glass in them was so dark, that anyone on the train could see out, but others couldn't see in.

"She is certainly impressive," the preacher whistled through his teeth, pushing his hat back a little on his head as if to get a better look at the *Scorpion Steam*.

"Impressive!" Drake roared with something close to boyish excitement. "She is magnificent! A true wonder!" Then, turning to look at the preacher, he added, "I'll wager she'll outrun any vampire."

"I'm not a betting man," the preacher breathed, looking at the train that hissed and spat before him. "And if I were, I'd only bet if the odds were heavily stacked in my favour – and they're not."

"I can see I'm yet to convince you, Preacher," Drake said, slapping one hand down firmly on the preacher's shoulder.

He looked at Drake's hand, and then fixed him with an icy stare. Smiling, Drake slid his hand slowly away. Then from behind me, I heard a sudden noise. I looked back to see several smartly dressed men step from the waiting room and onto the platform. Each of them was dressed in identical black suits and bowler hats, and they pushed before them a wooden trolley which carried a large black trunk. Without so much as looking at us, they pushed the trolley past like a row of smartly dressed porters. Immediately behind the tender was a huge carriage, which had a large door at one end. The porters, if that's what they were, passed this car and went to the next. They opened the door and between them, hoisted the trunks up into the carriage.

"What's in the boxes?" Harry asked Drake, who stood next to his private doctor.

"Supplies," he said, eyeing Harry. "You want to eat on this journey, don't you?"

Harry grunted and watched the trunks being carried onto the train. They were long, black, and made of metal.

"What's with the guys in the funny hats?" Zoe asked, the balls of her hands resting against her pistols in their holsters.

"Just some of my employees," Drake smiled at her.

"Are they coming along, too?" Louise asked, watching them carefully.

"No, no, they will be returning back to London," Drake smiled, moving towards one of the porters who was standing by the open carriage door. He leant forward so their cheeks were almost brushing. Drake said something that I was unable to hear and the porter looked at Drake, and then tipped the brim of his bowler hat as if acknowledging what had just been said to him.

The porter moved away and went to our horses, which still stood in the dust outside the station. "What are you doing?" Harry snapped as the porter started to lead his horse towards the train.

"There is no need for alarm, Turner," Drake said. "Your horse is being stabled on board the train. It will be well looked after."

The porter led the horse to the giant dropdown door in the carriage adjacent to the tender. He lowered the door like a drawbridge and led the horse inside. He reappeared moments later and went to the other horses outside the front of the station.

"Come, come," Drake said, ushering us away. "Let us all board the *Scorpion Steam*."

With his hands hanging beside his guns, the preacher looked at each of us in turn. Then we followed him and Drake along the platform and boarded the Scorpion Steam.

PART THREE

The Scorpion Steam

19

Spencer Drake led us through the many carriages that formed the *Scorpion Steam*. He took delight in showing us how grand the train was. And it was. Crimson silk curtains hung at every window, the floors were carpeted with deep rugs, and oil lamps hidden beneath the most finely cut china shades hung from every wall or stood on the tables that lined the dining car. I counted twelve cars in all. We had a berth each, and just like the rest of the train, our rooms were lavishly furnished. A narrow aisle ran the length of the train outside our rooms so we could pass from one carriage to another.

The very last carriage had a glass ceiling so you could look up into the night sky and wonder at the thousands of stars above. The end of the carriage opened out onto a small area where you could sit and watch the scenery pass by.

"This is the observation room," Drake said, a look of wonder on his face as he glanced up at the night sky through the clear roof. "Glorious, isn't it?"

"If you say so," Harry remarked with a shrug of his thick-set shoulders.

"It is beautiful," Zoe said glancing up. Drake glanced down at her and smiled, and I couldn't help but feel that there was more behind that smile than just friendliness. Zoe was stunningly beautiful and it hadn't gone unnoticed by Drake.

"What time do we eat?" Louise asked, guiding Zoe away from Drake, also noticing how he was looking at her.

"Dinner will be at midnight," Drake said, pulling his watch from a pocket on the front of his charcoal grey waistcoat.

"Midnight," I breathed, my own stomach beginning to rumble. I hadn't eaten since the eggs and pink pulp that morning.

Closing the front of the watch and placing it back into his pocket, Drake looked at us and said, "I'm sorry, but perhaps I should have mentioned before that I keep strange hours. It's my illness, you see. You won't see me very much during the day, if at all," he smiled. "I'll spend my days asleep, so please do not disturb me. If you need anything, please speak with one of my staff."

"Who?" Harry asked. "The doctor?"

"I'm afraid my doctor keeps the same odd hours that I do. He has to, you see, if he is to be at hand when I need him."

"You must pay him well," the preacher said.

Drake shot a quick smile at the preacher and said, "I do therefore apologise for the lateness of dinner, but as I have been resting all day, the hour suits me just fine." Then looking at each of us in turn, he added, "I hope that won't be a problem to any of you."

"No problem," Harry said back, and glanced at the preacher.

"Splendid," Drake smiled. He went to the door of the observation carriage, but before disappearing back into the rest of the train, he glanced back and said, "I have taken the liberty of providing each of the beautiful ladies a dress to wear to dinner tonight. You will find them in your rooms. I just thought – seeing as it is our first night aboard the *Scorpion Steam* – that such an occasion demanded that the ladies look divine."

Before any of us could say anything, he was gone, leaving us standing alone.

"I don't like him," Harry said. "He's so crooked he could swallow nails and spit out corkscrews."

"You said it," Zoe agreed, staring back up at the night sky in wonder.

"I was beginning to wonder if you didn't like him," Louise said.

"Who me?" Zoe said, smiling to herself. "Nah, not my type."

"What is your type?" Louise asked her.

"Someone who isn't always frigging smiling," and she glanced quickly across the carriage at Harry. He was looking out of the window, as the train started to slowly pull out of the station.

The carriage lurched, and there was the sound of chains rattling beneath us. The train rocked as we were pulled forward. The driver blew up on the horn and the noise was almost deafening. I left the carriage and stood on the small wooden area at the back of the train. The preacher joined me. He was quiet, as if thinking deeply about something.

"The light has gone," I said, watching the desolate station slip away into the distance and the dark.

"And so are those porters in the dumb hats," the preacher whispered thoughtfully, as he passed me one of his hand-rolled cigarettes.

20

My room, or more accurately described – carriage – was beautiful. It was as if Drake had spared no expense in providing the most up-to-date comforts and furnishings. There was a sofa, which was piled high with soft-looking pillows and lacy throws, which had been draped over the back and arms. There was an armchair, and next to this there was a small table with an oil lamp. Beside the lamp was a crystal decanter half filled with whiskey, a pitcher of water, and two glasses. There was a silver-framed mirror on the wall and several paintings of landscapes and mountain ranges. I didn't know where any of these places were. There was a bookshelf which was crammed full with leather-bound books. I ran my fingertips over the creased spines. Some appeared to have been written in French and Latin, but I was surprised to see a few books that I recognised. I took a copy of *Watchers at Night* by Rudyard Kipling from the shelf and carefully thumbed through the pages. They were tinted an off-white, and thicker than the pages in books from 2012. Then, gasping, I spotted *A Study in Scarlet* by Arthur Conan Doyle. I had lost count of how many times I had read that book. It was one of my favourites, and here I was, holding what was probably a first edition. Opening the book, I smelt the pages. I closed it and tucked it under my arm as I inspected the rest of the books. I found *The Pit and the Pendulum* by Edgar Allan Poe and Mary Shelley's *Frankenstein* among the collection.

I placed *A Study in Scarlet* on the table with the oil lamp and inspected the rest of the carriage. There was a small narrow door and opening it, I found myself looking into a berth. Against the wall, just below the window, was a bed. Not quite the size of a double, but bigger than a single. Laid across the bed was a red dress. I picked it up and the material felt soft, like silk. Just like the clothes of some of the women I had seen passing along the main street back in the town of Black Water Gap, the sleeves were decorated with pretty fluffs of lace, as was the hem of the skirt. There was a pair of woollen stockings and a pair of small leather ankle boots. I brushed the dress against my cheek and it felt wonderfully soft, like feathers.

With the train rocking from side to side, I took off

my clothes and slipped into the dress, stockings, and boots. The neck of the dress was low, but the cut of it pushed my breasts together, making them look bigger than they really were, and that was okay. Leaving the room, I went back and stood in front of the mirror. I let my hair fall loose about my shoulders, and as I looked in the mirror, I felt, for the first time since arriving in 1888, like a woman. I felt and looked as if I were going out somewhere special for the evening. The last time I had dressed up so nice was when Karl had taken me to the theatre for my birthday. The dress I'd been wearing that night hadn't been anything as grand as this. It had come from Next – I think. I wasn't one for going around in dresses and skirts at the first opportunity – but there were times when I liked to look nice – feel special. So, turning around and around on the spot, I let the dress swish about my calves as I sang the song 'Last Friday Night' by Katy Perry.

With my head in a spin and feeling dizzy, I slumped into the armchair and lit the cigarette that the preacher had given to me. Since arriving in 1888, I laughed for the first time. Only I could end up on a steam train racing across the old west, wearing the most beautiful dress I had ever seen, with a library of books probably worth millions, singing a Katy Perry song, and smoking a cigarette rolled by a preacher. Once I had my fit of giggles under control, and with the cigarette dangling from the corner of my mouth, I went back to the berth and looked down at my guns.

Would I need them at dinner tonight? I wondered. Besides, where was I going to put them? They didn't exactly match my long flowing dress. Deciding that I wouldn't need them, I put them down again and made to leave. Then stopping at the door, I took the small bottle of holy water, hitched up my skirt, and tucked it into the neck of my stocking. Why I had thought to do that, I didn't know. It was like that other me – the one who could shoot, fight, and ride – the one who'd kept me alive so far, was watching out for me. I left my room and went in search of the others.

I made my way along the narrow aisles that stretched along outside the other rooms and berths. The train rocked from side to side and several times I had to place the flat of my hand against the wall to stop myself from toppling over. Reaching the end of the carriage, I opened the door and was hit by a rush of cold air. I looked down and could see the iron coupling which kept the carriages joined together. There was a small step that I had to make to get to the next carriage. Looking into the gap, I could see the ballast and sleepers racing away below. Gripping the rail, I stepped across the gap just as the train rocked violently. I gasped as I stumbled forward. Then, just as I feared that I was going to lose my footing, someone gripped my arm. I looked up to see that it was Harry who had taken hold of me.

He pulled me roughly into the adjoining carriage. I tried to squirm my arm free of his grip, but just like he had on the riverbank, he had hold of me tightly.

"You can let go of me now," I said, trying to avoid his stare, but I just couldn't. His grey eyes looked particularly dark tonight.

"Are you sure you're okay?" he asked, his voice as gruff and unfriendly as usual.

"I'm sure," I said, yanking my arm free.

"Well, if you're sure," he said, that arrogant grin forming on his lips.

"What is your problem?" I hissed, just wanting to knock that smug look from his face.

"No problem," he smiled, and I caught his eyes – just for a second – wander down to my overexposed chest.

He does like me, I thought. But then again, didn't most men find their eyes wandering at the sight of a big pair of breasts? *I could have looked like King Kong's auntie and he still would have looked*, I thought, pushing the idea that he found me attractive from my mind. And what did I care anyway? The guy was a jerk.

I pushed my way past Harry and opened the door which led into the dining car. The others had already gathered there. Harry came in behind me and closed the door, shutting out the cold. Flames flickered from the candles which had been placed in the centre of a large round table in the middle of the carriage.

Mirrors seemed to hang on every free space of the carriage wall. It was difficult not to look in any direction and not see your reflection staring back at you. Each mirror was framed in silver, and as there were many mirrors, there was just as much silver. The knives and forks, which had been neatly placed at the table, dazzled along with the silver drinking goblets and condiments. Even the napkins were fastened together with silver rings.

"Why so many mirrors?" Zoe asked, checking herself out in one.

Drake approached her from behind and peered at his own reflection over her shoulder. "Why have paintings adorn the walls, when we ourselves can create such beautiful pieces of art?" he smiled at her.

Zoe blushed, her pale cheeks filling with colour.

As if relishing her embarrassment, Drake leaned in closer to her and breathed, "Some say that those who don't have souls don't reflect, but your reflection is so clear – so wonderful; it's like I can see into your very soul, Zoe Edgar."

Although Zoe was smiling back at him in the mirror, I saw her fingers reach up for the pistols she had hanging from the harness over the emerald-coloured dress she was wearing. Unlike me, Zoe had felt the need to bring her guns to dinner.

I glanced over at Louise, who stood next to the preacher. She wore a pale blue dress that was similar to mine. Her dark hair coiled around her shoulders and shone against her cream-coloured skin.

"Please, let us eat," Drake said, sitting at the table alongside his personal doctor.

Once everyone was seated, we were joined in the dining car by several waiters, who all wore pristine white aprons about their waists. They placed a silver plate in front of each of us. I looked down at mine and could see a slab of meat. It looked so undercooked and raw it swam in a pool of its own blood. I prodded at it with my fork and turned up my nose.

"More elk?" I said, more to myself than the others seated around the table.

"Beef," Drake corrected me, and I looked across the table to see blood oozing from the meat on his plate.

The waiters returned with china bowls that were crammed with steaming piles of potatoes and green vegetables. With silver spoons, they heaped the food onto our plates.

"That's enough," I said, raising my hand, watching one of the waiters place a fourth potato onto the plate before me.

The waiters disappeared, and picking up a bottle of wine from the centre of the table, Drake filled the silver goblets. I looked back at him across the table and watched as he then cut the meat on his plate. Blood dribbled down his chin and he dabbed it away with a napkin. None of the others seemed to be bothered by the undercooked meat as they all set about it. I know some people like their steak raw – but this just took the piss. The lumps of meat looked as if they had just been hacked off the cow and served up.

I pushed the meat to the edge of my plate and cut one of the potatoes in half.

"So what's the real reason for all the mirrors?" Louise asked Drake, and then took a sip of her wine. "You never really answered Zoe's question."

"Vanity," he smiled at her.

"Why don't you cut the crap, Drake," Harry suddenly spoke up over a mouthful of the red meat. "If all of these mirrors are some kind of test to see if we're vampires, then you're wasting your time."

Drake clapped his hands together and chuckled. "Very good, Turner. You're sharper than one might first suspect." Then, shrugging his shoulders, he added, "Can you blame me? Can any of you blame me? I'm setting off into the mountains with a group of so-called vampire hunters. I just wanted to make sure I wasn't going to become *the hunted*."

Hearing this, I brushed my fingers over the tiny bottle of holy water I had fixed down the neck of my tights.

"We're not vampires," the preacher hissed, his eyes now brighter than they were earlier. "But what about you?"

"That's ridiculous," Drake scoffed. "Me, a vampire? Why, you have seen my reflection in the mirror."

"And you have seen ours," the preacher reminded him. "But yet, you still suspect us."

"I know a way that we can settle this," I spoke up. They all turned to look at me.

"How?" the preacher snapped, harsher than I believe he intended. I knew that he was pissed at Drake.

Producing the bottle of holy water, I placed it on the table. Each of them looked at it. "It's holy water I took from the chapel back in Black Water Gap." I looked around the table and could see each of them eyeing the bottle.

Slowly, I pulled the cork from the neck and poured some of the holy water into my glass. I passed it to Louise, who sat next to me. She looked at me, then down at the bottle. She took it and poured a little into her glass. She then handed it to Zoe who poured some of the water out and handed it to Harry.

"It's nice to know you're trusted," he moaned. Then, looking across the table at me, he poured some of the holy water into his glass, just like the others had.

Next to him sat the doctor, who without hesitation, tipped the bottle and emptied some of it into his glass. Drake took it from him, and without taking his eyes off of the preacher, he poured half of what was left in the bottle into his glass. He then handed it to the preacher. With the bottle hovering over his glass, he looked around the table at each of us and emptied it.

Taking up his glass, and with a smile, Drake held out his hand and said, "Good health, ladies and gentlemen."

There was a tension in the room, and my heart started to speed up. I slipped my free hand beneath the table and rested it against my thigh, searching for my guns. And then I remembered they weren't there.

Why hadn't I brought them? I cursed as I surveyed the room. At once, my eyes started to measure the distance that I sat from the others. My mind began to calculate which of them posed the greatest threat. I looked for anything that I could use as a weapon.

Then as one, we lifted our glasses, clinked them against Drake's, and drank the holy water.

With our glasses poised at our lips, we eyed each other around the table, as if half expecting one of us to start convulsing, leaking smoke from our eyeballs, or foaming at the mouth. But nothing happened. It was then I noticed the preacher hadn't drunk from his glass.

"Drink up," Drake smiled nervously across the table at the preacher.

The preacher ignored him and stared at Louise. With the speed of a rattlesnake, I palmed my knife and held it in my lap beneath the table.

"Be a good fellow and drink up like the rest of us," Drake pushed the preacher again.

"I do not need to be tested by you," the preacher

said coolly, turning his attention from Louise and back to Drake. "I'm no vampire."

"Then you won't mind drinking up," the doctor said, pushing his chair back from the table and standing up. He brandished a large silver crucifix at the preacher. The doctor's chair hadn't even stopped sliding back across the floor when the preacher was on his feet. His gun was drawn, and the end of the barrel was just inches from the doctor's face.

"Show some respect," the preacher whispered. "That crucifix you so happily wave around isn't some kind of good luck charm."

Drake gently rested his hand on the doctor's forearm and said, "Marcus, please, I know you are only trying to do your duty by protecting me, but sit down."

With the crucifix still held tightly in his fist, the doctor righted his chair and sat back at the table. Then looking at the preacher, Drake said, "You can hardly blame my friend for being jumpy if you won't drink the water."

"I don't need to prove anything to you," the preacher said holstering his gun as quickly as he had drawn it. "There is someone far greater than you who judges me."

"That might be so," Drake smiled again, "but I don't have your faith. As you said yourself, Preacher, I'm like the Disciple, Thomas. I need to see wounds before I believe."

"I'll show you a wound," the preacher hissed,

unbuttoning his shirt. "I'll show you my burden." His shirt fell open down the front, and burnt into his chest was the shape of a cross. The scar was white, the skin around it mauve and raw-looking as if it had never quite healed. Snatching up the glass with the holy water in it, he threw back his head and drank.

Trying to hide a look of shock, Drake mustered a smile. Looking at the preacher, he said, "Please, take a seat. I meant no offence . . . "

Slamming the glass down on the table, the preacher glared at Drake and whispered, "Be careful what you pray for – there is no such thing as an unanswered prayer." Then he was gone, striding from the dining car. Lifting up the hems of her long flowing dress, Louise got up from the table and followed him.

"More drink, anyone?" Drake smiled at us, filling his glass with the red wine.

21

I hadn't felt like eating that lump of red meat before, but now the atmosphere in the room was so frosty, my appetite went altogether. Harry threw his napkin onto his plate and I watched some of the blood from the meat soak into it. He pushed his chair back from the table and left the dining car without saying a word to anyone.

I glanced at Zoe, who drank the last of her wine in one quick gulp and stood up.

"Excuse me," she said, "but I think I'll go to bed now. Thank you for dinner, it was very interesting." Then like the others, she was bolting through the dining car door.

"And then there were three," Drake smiled at me and the doctor.

"I guess," I said, wondering if I had caused the scene by doing the whole holy water thing.

Setting his glass down, Drake looked across the table at me, and the candlelight flickered in his eyes.

"You're not like the others," he said.

"How come?" I asked him.

"They seem to be so . . . how can I explain," he mused. Then gathering his thoughts he went on. "They seem to be so uptight."

"I hadn't noticed," I lied, not wanting to start slagging off my friends.

Friends? Were they? I wondered. I didn't really know anything about the preacher and the others. But still, I wouldn't say anything bad about them, as they had given me food and shelter – taken me in – since arriving in 1888.

Changing the subject, Drake said, "So, Miss Carter, do you believe in these Vrykolakas – these *vampires?*"

"Yes," I said looking straight back at him through the candlelight.

"So you've seen one then?" the doctor asked, sitting forward at the table with interest.

"I'm not sure," I said, remembering the man who had strangled me on the train.

"You're not sure?" Drake asked, lighting a cigarette. He dropped the match onto his plate where it floated in the bloody-red gravy. "Does this have something to do with faith, the faith that the preacher likes to talk about so much?"

"No," I said, shaking my head. "I've always believed in the existence of vampires. I don't need to see one to believe."

"So it is a matter of faith then?" the doctor asked me.

Ignoring the doctor, I looked at the cigarette smouldering between Drake's fingers and said, "Can I have one of those?"

Without saying anything, Drake slid a silver box and a book of matches across the table with his fingertips. I took one of the cigarettes from the box and lit it. With smoke curling up from the corner of my mouth, I said, "I've just always known that vampires exist – I don't know why."

"Tell me about this vampire who you thought you saw," Drake said, reaching across the table and refilling my empty glass with wine.

I lifted my glass and took a sip. The wine was sweet. Drake and his doctor stared at me from across the table and I could sense their eagerness as they waited for me to start talking.

"I followed this man down onto the tube," I said.

"The tube?" the doctor asked, looking confused.

Shit! Did they know about the tube? Had the London Underground system even been built in 1888? I'm sure parts of it had been. I could remember being taken on a school trip to the London Transport Museum and seeing pictures of wooden carriages being pulled through the tunnels by steam engines. My teacher, Mrs. Plum, had been trying to get us to imagine how suffocating the tunnels would have been with all that smoke and very little ventilation. I wished I had paid more attention now, instead of sneaking away to the bathroom to have a sneaky smoke with my friends.

"The trains that travel underground?" I said tentatively.

"Oh," the doctor said, sideways glancing at Drake. "You call it the tube?"

"No, not really," I said, trying to cover over my mistake. "It was a little joke of my father's. He said it was like riding around in a big tube underground."

"How very inventive," Drake smiled. "Please, continue."

"Well, I chased this man down into the underground and he took a train on the Circle Line . . . " I started.

"Don't you mean the Inner Circle?" the doctor corrected me again with a frown.

"That's the one," I said, and drew on my cigarette.

"Why where you following him?" Drake asked me.

"Because I suspected him of being a killer," I said flatly.

"That was a very brave thing to do, Miss Carter," Drake shot back, the flames from the candlelight casting long shadows, like cuts, across his face.

"Or stupid," I tried to joke, wishing that perhaps I hadn't started this conversation with him now. How long would it be before I tripped myself up again and mentioned something which was out of place and out of time? I sat quietly for a moment, wondering if it was too late to make my apologies and slip away to my room.

"Please continue, Miss Carter, with your most arresting narrative," Drake said, crushing out his cigarette with his thumb and forefinger.

"I followed this man onto the train," I continued as they watched me from the other side of the table. "I couldn't see him at first. The train was empty – there were no other passengers. I searched the carriages, and just when I thought that perhaps he hadn't boarded the train after all, he was behind me. He wrapped his arm around my throat and it felt as if he was strangling me."

"His face? Did you see it?" Drake asked, his eyes almost seeming to glow.

"No," I said. "I started to lose consciousness and then . . . " I trailed off.

"Then what, Miss Carter?" the doctor probed.

"I woke up here, just on the outskirts of Black Water Gap," I said, feeling a little relieved that I had told my story – in part, anyway.

"And the preacher?" Drake asked.

"What about him?"

"Did you know him before arriving here?"

"No," I said, blowing cigarette smoke into the air.

159

The train listed right then left, as we rattled over a set of points. "He was just there when I woke up. It was like he found me."

"Most interesting," Drake said, glancing at the doctor, then back at me.

"This man you were chasing," Drake said, taking another cigarette from the silver box, "you said you suspected him of being a killer. Who did he murder?"

"Four women," I said. "Probably five. He killed them in the most barbaric of ways. He cut them open, removed their intestines, and performed grotesque mutilations upon their bodies."

"There is only one killer who has such a *modus operandi*," Drake whispered. "You were following Jack the Ripper onto that train."

I wanted to tell him that I wasn't. I wanted to tell him the man I was chasing committed his murders one-hundred-and-twenty-four years after the Ripper's last murder, but in my heart, I wondered even if I was sure of that. Knowing I would probably regret what I was about to say next, I took a large mouthful of wine. My head swam and I said, "I think he followed me here."

"Who did? What do you mean, child?" the doctor asked, confused.

"Jack – I think like I came here, he is here, too," I said.

I saw Drake and the doctor look at one another, and

then back at me. "What makes you say such a wild thing?" Drake asked me.

"I found this newspaper just before we left town," I started to explain, my head now feeling a little woozy. "A woman was butchered in the last few days in a town called Crows Ranch. She was a prostitute, just like the other victims – the women who were murdered back in Whitechapel. But there were other similarities, too. The killer cut her throat and removed her internal organs, just like the Ripper did with his second victim, Annie Chapman."

"You seem to have taken a personal interest in the killings of the Ripper," Drake said.

I couldn't tell him that I studied the murders as part of my criminology degree. I very much doubted that young women in the Whitechapel area of London would have been so privileged back in 1888.

"I read the newspapers," I told him.

"So it would appear," the doctor whispered thoughtfully.

"Are you suggesting that he brought you here?"

"I'm not suggesting anything," I said, standing up and feeling my legs wobble beneath me. I'd had way too much wine. "I'm going to bed."

"If you could spare us just one moment more of your time, Miss Carter," Drake asked, as I headed for the door. "I'd like to ask you just one further question."

"What's that?" I asked, peering back at him.

"Do you believe that Jack the Ripper is a vampire?" he asked, and again, that smile played across his perfect lips.

"I don't know what to believe anymore," I said, and then turning, I left the dining car.

22

My brain felt as if it was going around and around on a carousel, and I felt like getting some air to clear my head. I teetered down the passageways outside the other berths and made my way to the observation chamber. I planned to stand on that little balcony and watch the night sky full of its stars pass by overhead. The train made a constant *clackety-clack* sound beneath me as it raced along.

I reached the observation carriage with its glass roof and pushed open the door. Harry was sitting in one of the seats and looking up at the stars. Hoping he hadn't seen me, I wheeled right around as the door hit me in the arse. Gathering up my skirt, I started back through the door.

"You can stay," I heard him say. "I don't bite."

I stopped and let the door swing closed. Taking a deep breath and trying to focus through the groggy feeling in my head, I made my way over to where he was sitting.

Without saying anything, he gestured to the seat opposite him, and I sat down before I fell down.

"Whiskey?" he said, and I could see that there were two glasses and a bottle of the stuff on the table before him.

"No, I'm okay . . . " I started, but before I could finish, he had splashed some of the whiskey into the empty glass.

"Can I have some water with that?" I asked.

"Just ran out of water," he said, looking at me. "What keeps you up so late?"

"I've been talking to Drake and his doctor friend," I said.

"That must have been interesting for you," he groaned, then took a sip of his whiskey.

"Very," I half-smiled.

"What did you find to talk about for so long?" he asked me nonchalantly, but I knew he was more than interested.

"This and that," I said, the carriage swaying, and I couldn't tell if it was due to the train passing over points, or me being half pissed.

"You're not like the rest of us," Harry remarked, sitting back in his chair and watching me.

"That's what Drake said," and his stare made me feel uncomfortable.

"What else did Drake have to say?" he asked me, his eyes never leaving mine.

"He wanted to know how I came to be here," I told him. Then picking up the whiskey and taking a sip, I added, "And do you know what? I don't even know myself."

"That whole memory loss thing?" he asked me, with a disbelieving look.

In the warm glow of the oil lamps fixed to the carriage walls he looked so fucking hot, with his messy, sandy-coloured hair, stubble covering the lower half of his face like a shadow, and those hard, cold eyes. I hated myself for thinking about him like that, because the guy was a complete dickhead, so I looked away.

"Is it that you can't remember, or are you hiding something – keeping a secret?" Harry asked. His voice was still gruff but it had mellowed somehow.

"Like I've already said, the last thing I remember was chasing that man onto a train, and then finding myself here," I told him, looking up at the night sky.

"It's a secret then," Harry said.

"And so what if it was?" I snapped, casting my eyes down at him. "Aren't I allowed to have a secret? It's not as if you aren't keeping plenty of your own."

"What's that s'posed to mean?" he said right back.

"I saw what you did to that bear the other day," I

165

told him. "I saw how fast you ran along the river-bank . . . "

"You don't know what you're talking about," he said dismissing me with a wave of his hand.

"I know what I saw," I insisted.

"You're imagining things," he spat. "You were under-water. How do you know what you really saw?"

With the whiskey only making my thoughts and memory even foggier, I couldn't now be sure of what I had seen. And although the whiskey and the wine clouded my thoughts, it also gave me courage, so I said, "I didn't imagine you with your hand gripping my arse."

"Crap!" Harry spat, spraying whiskey from his lips. "I wasn't grabbing your ass."

"Yeah, you were," I said back. "You couldn't keep your eyes off me." I knew this wasn't actually true, as I vaguely remembered him strutting off up the riverbank without so much as a glance back at me. But it made me feel good to try and get the better of him.

"I haven't been able to take my eyes off you?" he gasped. "It's you who hasn't been able to keep your eyes off me, doll."

"Yeah?" I snapped in disbelief.

"You know it," he said smugly, and I had to do everything in my power not to smash his face in.

"We'll see about that," I said, staggering to my feet. I wobbled my way out onto the balcony and a rush of cold air hit my face like a sharp slap. I drew in a mouthful of cold night air and it made me feel better – but not much.

Clackety-clack, clackety-clack, clackety-clack, the train went all around me as it lurched to and fro. I teetered to my right and fumbled for the rail to steady myself, but lost my grip.

"Steady there," Harry said from behind me. Then, he was holding on to me.

"See," I mumbled. "You just can't leave me alone."

"I'm just trying to stop your sorry ass from falling over the side," he said, holding me tight.

I looked up into his face and said, "See, there you go, talking about my arse again."

Looking down at me, Harry said, "Why do you have to be so difficult?"

"I'm not difficult," I said, secretly enjoying being held by him again. I giggled and said, "I'm nice."

"Who needs nice," he said with that grim look.

"You like nice," I said, shifting in his arms so my face was closer to his. I might have been drunk, but not so much so that I hadn't realised he hadn't released me yet, even though I was no longer in danger of falling from the train.

With his arms tightening around my waist like a snake, he brought his lips within touching distance of mine. I could smell the whiskey on his breath. Then someone spoke.

"I'm sorry, I thought I was the only one awake," the voice said.

Letting go of me, Harry looked around and I followed his stare. Zoe was standing in the open doorway of the carriage. She looked surprised to find me in Harry's arms.

"Is everything okay?" she asked.

"Fine," Harry said, heading back towards the table, where he picked up his whiskey glass and poured himself another shot.

"I think I need to get some sleep," I said, touching my forehead with my fingertips. Part of me was glad that Zoe had come in when she had, as I would have only regretted kissing Harry when I was sober the following morning. But there was this other part of me that wished we had kissed. There was a fluttering in my stomach, and I knew it hadn't been caused by the drink.

I carefully navigated my way across the carriage, glancing at Harry as I went. He looked back at me and I wondered if he felt the same as I did.

"Goodnight," I said reaching the door, leaving Harry and Zoe alone.

23

I closed the door to my room and wobbled over towards the armchair. Using it as a support, I pulled off my clothes, kicking them away. Naked, I stumbled into my berth and fell onto the bed. The constant motion of the train did nothing to stop my head from spinning. I lay on my back and listened to the sound of the train rumbling across the desert. But in the constant *clackety-clack* sound of the train's giant wheels passing along the tracks, I realised I could hear other noises. It was the sound of two people making love, and the sound was coming from the carriage next to mine – the carriage that the preacher and Louise shared.

"Don't they ever stop shagging?" I giggled aloud.

I lay in the dark and listened to them. The sounds of their moans and groans grew steadily louder and more frequent in the dark. I don't know if it was because I was drunk – but to hear them kind of turned me on. Then came the sound of smashing and crashing, as if furniture was being thrown about their berth. I could hear Louise shrieking with delight and the preacher groaning, as if in uncontrollable ecstasy.

"Louise was right, the preacher is an animal," I giggled again as I lay and listened to them.

The train rocked left then right, and I wondered if it wasn't their overly enthusiastic lovemaking that had nearly brought the train off its rails. I closed my eyes to the soundtrack of their constant groaning and sighing and thought of Karl. It had been a long time since I'd had sex with him – or with anyone, for that matter. I could picture him in my head, his smooth good looks, black hair, and clean-shaven chin. I tried to remember the last time that we had had sex, but couldn't quite remember. With the sound of the preacher's and Louise's sex marathon taking place next door, I slipped my hand between my legs and slowly started to stroke myself. The whole world felt as if it was spinning around me. As I slid my fingers a little faster, I tried to picture Karl in my mind's eye, but it was like he was hidden behind a wall of mist. However hard I tried to conjure an image of him having sex with me, he just remained a faint, distant shadow. I raised my knees and parted my legs slightly and rubbed my fingers faster as the sounds from the berth next door intensified.

Then out of the fog that swirled around my mind, I saw Karl step clear of it – but it wasn't Karl – it was Harry. He came towards me and wrapped his strong arm around my waist. I was naked, just like I had been on the riverbank. I could feel his hand again. But this time, instead of letting it rest just above the groove of my buttocks, he worked his fingers between my legs and I let them enter me. I squeezed my eyes shut tighter still and arched my back as I moved my fingers faster and faster. I gasped as I suddenly felt my hand being brushed away. I half opened my eyes to see Harry kneeling over me.

"Keep your eyes closed," he breathed, bringing his face above mine. Like I had in the observation carriage, I could smell whiskey on his breath.

"What are you doing?" I gasped as he slid a finger inside of me and started to push it slowly up and down.

"Shhhhh," he breathed in my ear. "Keep your eyes closed. Whatever you do, don't look at me."

"Why not?" I sighed, as he eased another of his fingers into me, moving them faster.

"Because if you don't keep your eyes closed – if you look at me, then this becomes real," he whispered. "It stops being a fantasy."

"But what if I want it to be real?" I breathed, taking hold of his hand between my legs and working it faster.

"Just enjoy it for what it is," he said, then closed his mouth over one of my nipples.

Like he told me, I kept my eyes closed, fearing that if I opened them, the fantasy would come to an end, as would the burning feeling of excitement that was building deep within me. I didn't want that to stop – not ever. With me guiding his hand faster and faster, he buried his head between my breasts and covered them in rough kisses. I could feel his stubble needle my flesh, and the fingers of my free hand slid through his hair. My nipples hardened, and he nipped at them with his teeth.

"That hurts," I gasped.

"You don't know what pain is," he whispered, and ran his tongue over the flat of my stomach. I felt the tip of it probe my navel and I arched my back, raising my hips. In this position he could slide his fingers deeper into me and I cried out as my body seemed to spasm from my head right down all the way through to my toes.

With my ankles digging into the bed and my fists gripping the sheets, I let him take control of the speed in which he pleasured me. His strong fingers worked faster and faster and I shuddered out of control. My heart raced so fast and loud in my chest that I thought it was going to explode. His fingers moved faster inside of me, and I tried to hold back the inevitable – enjoying the unbearable sensation so much – not wanting it to end, afraid that I may never feel like this again. When I couldn't bear it any longer, I let go and the orgasm was so intense that I bit into my lower lip until I had drawn blood.

Harry stroked my breasts with the tips of his fingers, then lunging forward he kissed me. His tongue explored the inside of my mouth as I forced mine into his. He lay on top of me, and I could feel his naked body. His cock felt hard against my stomach.

Breaking our kiss, and keeping my eyes closed, I whispered in his ear, "Take me from behind."

"Only if you do as I say and keep your eyes closed," he whispered back. Then, rolling me over onto all fours, he knelt on the bed behind me. Harry gripped my hips with his hands and pulled me towards him. I murmured as he entered me, and dropped my shoulders. I buried my face in the pillow so I couldn't see him. It felt as if I had blindfolded myself somehow. With his hands gripping my arse, he worked his hips backwards and forwards, slowly pushing himself in and sliding out of me.

I gripped the sheets and cried out as he slowly took me. For the first time in my life, I truly understood why Sally had screamed so much. I wanted to now. I had never felt so turned on in my life. The train rocked back and forth and it was like Harry had fallen in sync with the motion of it. Karl would have been all over and done with by now and I would have been lying on my back, smoking a cigarette, while he snored beside me; but Harry had only just started.

Still inside of me, Harry reached around and cupped my breasts in his hands. He squeezed them, rubbed them, and pulled at them. I cried out again, and it was then I noticed that his hands felt bigger somehow. They felt coarser than they had before. He ran them up from my breasts and around my throat, where he gently squeezed. I felt long fingernails scrape at the flesh around my throat, as he pushed harder and faster into me. His groans behind me sounded deep and throaty, like some kind of beast.

Turning my head to one side against the pillow, I decided to open my eyes just a fraction to look back at him. Harry sensed what I was about to do, so taking his strong hands from around my throat; he entwined them in my long hair and shoved my face back into the pillow so I couldn't look at him as promised.

"Shut your eyes. I'm not going to hurt you," he said, and his voice, like his groans of pleasure, sounded different somehow – deeper – stronger.

I didn't feel scared as such, I felt too horny to feel fear. I'd always wished that Karl had been more adventurous. Little did I know I would have to travel back to the year 1888 and get laid by a moody cowboy to find such pleasure. There was nothing to be scared of, just like Harry had said, this was my fantasy and I was going to enjoy it.

"Harder," I cried out. "I know you want to."

As if what I had said had pushed a button in him

somewhere, Harry began to push faster and harder into me. I raised my arse as high as I could so he could force himself deeper within me. With both of us shouting out and groaning with unbearable pleasure, and sounding just like the preacher and Louise had in the berth next door, I worked my hips up and down in time with Harry's thrusts. I wanted him as much as he wanted me.

I could feel an intense throbbing sensation between my legs which was only growing stronger and hotter as we moved faster and faster against each other. I felt Harry spasm violently behind me and he cried out – his voice almost sounding like a deep growl. My heart sped up – racing deep within me. Then the sense of pressure I had been feeling gave way and my body rippled with an uncontrollable series of spasms, the inside of my thighs suddenly wet. It was like nothing else in the world mattered, I just wanted the unbearable feeling of bliss to carry on for ever – I didn't want it to stop. With my whole body trembling and covered in sweat, I collapsed onto my front. I lay there, that feeling slowly ebbing away. My heart started to slow down, I breathed deeply. The room continued to spin, yet I felt tired and the most relaxed I could ever remember feeling, even though my arms and legs were shaking.

I rolled onto my back and whispered, "Can I open my eyes now?"

There was only silence.

"Harry?" I breathed, still trying to catch my breath. Silence.

Slowly, I opened my eyes. I peered about in the darkness, but couldn't see Harry. There was just me. *Perhaps he had gone into the other room to find more whiskey?* I wondered. I wrapped the bed sheet around my shoulders, and with my legs still wobbling beneath me, I made my way into the adjoining room.

"Harry?" I whispered again, but he wasn't there. I was alone.

I dropped into the armchair and felt a complete fool. Harry hadn't been in my room at all. We hadn't just shared the best sex I'd ever had. I had done that to myself, lying there drunk, listening to the preacher and Louise hump in the carriage next door. The sex with Harry had just been another part of this fantasy. The fantasy I was creating for myself as I lay half-dead on the carriage of that train, beneath the London of 2012.

Then, as I got up to stagger back to my berth, I noticed something. With the sheet wrapped around me, I lurched across my room to the door, which was now ajar. I was sure that I had closed it; I was convinced I had. I pulled the door open and looked in both directions up the carriage way, half expecting – hoping – to find Harry. There was no one there.

I closed the door.

24

I woke up feeling as if someone had buried a pickaxe in the front of my head. My tongue felt as thick as a rug and my mouth tasted of road kill. I sat up, at first not remembering where I was. I looked about the small berth and then remembered – I was on that train. But there was something wrong – it wasn't moving. That constant rocking and rolling and *clackety-clacking* had stopped. Shielding my eyes with one hand, I pulled back the curtain an inch and peered out. I didn't know what time it was, but the sun was low in the sky and its light was weak.

We appeared to have stopped at some remote railway station. A sign above the entrance read "Silent Rest". From what I could see through the small window beside my bed, was more dust, cactus plants and . . . *Harry*!

He passed beneath my window and I closed the gap in the curtain.

"Oh, my God!" I cried out, as memories of what had happened between us the night before flooded my mind.

Did we really do that? I wondered, my cheeks flushing hot. Did I really tell him to take me from behind?!

"What was I thinking of?" I breathed, clapping my hands over my face. "How am I ever gonna look at him again?"

Slowly separating my fingers, I peered through them as I then remembered opening my eyes and discovering that he hadn't been in my room at all last night. It had all been a drunken fantasy. But had it? Quick flashes of memory sliced their way through my hangover as I remembered discovering that the door to my room had been left open.

"Someone had been in here with me," I said aloud, desperate to convince myself. But then again, I'd been so drunk last night, I could've easily left the door open myself. I couldn't be sure of anything.

"Sammy, wake up!" I shouted at myself, slapping my temples with the flat of my hands. "C'mon, you can do it! You can wake up back in 2012 if you really think about it. C'mon!" I closed my eyes and thought of all the things that I missed from back home and shouted them out loud. "Twitter! Facebook! iPod! Rihanna! Macky-Dee's! L'Oreal!"

"What's iPod?" someone asked.

I snapped open my eyes to find Zoe standing in the doorway of my berth and looking at me with an odd look. She was holding a silver tray in her hands.

"What's iPod?" she asked me again.

"Something I could do with right now," I gasped, shocked to see her standing there.

"So, what is iPod?" she asked, coming and sitting at the foot of my bed and placing the tray on her lap.

I looked at her; the whole situation was so surreal that I started to laugh.

"What's so funny?" she asked with a half-smile on her pretty face.

"You, sitting there, asking me what is iPod," I said. "iPod isn't an *is* it's a *what*."

"What?" she said, her smile now fading, wondering if I was laughing at her?

"It doesn't matter," I said, still trying to mask my own smile. But to hear her say the name of an object which wouldn't be invented for another hundred years or more seemed so weird. I looked at her sitting on the end of my bed, her rough woven denims, boots, blue shirt, gun belt with revolvers fastened to her thighs. She must be the only cowgirl in 1888 who was ever going to mutter the word *iPod*.

But it wasn't really funny. It was sad because I was either really trapped in 1888, going mad, or both. Without even really knowing I was about to do it, I started to cry. My body shook as I wrapped the sheet about me and pressed the heels of my hands over my eyes. I felt Zoe get up from the end of the bed, and slip her arm around my shoulders.

"Don't cry," Zoe said, squeezing me tight. "What's wrong?"

"It's nothing," I sniffed.

"You can talk to me," Zoe said. "I promise I won't tell anyone."

"I shouldn't be here," I snivelled. "I'm from another place."

"I know," Zoe said. "You're from England. But that isn't so bad, is it? I mean, you speak funny and all, but that doesn't bother me."

"Thanks," I laughed between my sobs. "I don't fit in here – I don't even know what I'm doing here. I don't know who I am anymore. It's like I'm different somehow," I blurted out.

"I felt like that once," she said softly.

"You did?" I asked, taking my hands from over my eyes and looking at her.

"Sure," she said, looking back at me.

"What happened?" I asked, wondering if she was like me in some way – had come from someplace else.

"The preacher saved me," she said thoughtfully. "I was lost, and then found."

"What do you mean by that?" I asked, wiping the tears from my cheeks.

"My whole family was killed by vampires," she said, her eyes looking haunted, as if reliving some terrible nightmare. "They came in the night as we slept in our beds. I woke up to the sounds of my mother's screams. I was little at the time, eleven, I think, it seems like such a long time ago now. My older brother, Jack, came running into my room, and taking me by the hand, he dragged me away to the barn where he hid me. He went back to help my mother and father, but those vampires killed him, too."

"How can you be so sure?" I asked her, shocked by what she was telling me.

"I hid in the barn three days. I was too scared to come out," she whispered, still looking away. "It rained really badly one night and I remember feeling so thirsty. My lips were cracked and dry so I licked up the rain which dribbled in from beneath the barn door. In the end, I was so hungry I had to leave my hiding place. But then I wished I hadn't. I wished that I'd starved in that barn, because if I had never left it, I wouldn't have seen their bodies. The vampires had left my family strewn across the ground by the well. Their throats had been ripped out, and their bodies were just empty shells. I shooed away the crows that pecked at them. I wanted to bury their bodies, but I couldn't, I couldn't bring myself to touch them. I took some stale bread and a flask of water from the house and left the farm and never went back. Filthy, tired, and scared, I staggered out into the desert. I remember counting three moon rises, so I think I walked for three days. On the fourth, I collapsed in the searing heat. With my eyes half open, I prayed for Jesus to come and take me away, to take me to him. Then with my eyes closing upon the world, I saw a figure riding towards me out of the desert. Through the wavering heat that shimmered off the dusty ground, I could see the figure was dressed in black. At first I thought it was the devil, not Jesus, who had come to save me. Then with my eyes closing, I looked up to see that it wasn't the devil, it was a preacher man." Then turning to face me, Zoe ended her story by saying, "The preacher saved me, Sammy, and he will save you, too – if you just have faith in him."

I thought of how I had woken in the desert to find the preacher standing on the rocks, the tails of his black coat billowing out behind him like some kind of apparition. "How can he save me? What is he going to save me from?" I asked Zoe, as she slipped her arm from around my shoulders and stood up.

"The vampires, of course," she said, picking up the tray which she had left at the foot of the bed. Then, as if changing the subject, she smiled at me and said, "I brought you some food."

"Not more elk," I groaned.

"Bacon and eggs," she smiled, pulling away the cloth that covered the food.

I took the tray from her and smiled back. "Thank you, Zoe," I said, then added, "Why have we stopped?"

"The driver says that the train needs to take on more water and coal before we head into the mountains. This is the last chance we will get. After that it's just . . . " and she trailed off.

"Just what?" I asked, cutting the eggs in half with my fork.

"The preacher says we're heading into Hell," Zoe said, heading for the door. Then she stopped, and reaching into her back pocket, she smiled, "Drake has toothbrushes!"

She threw the small wooden brush at me and I snatched it out of the air with a flick of my wrist and I looked at it. The teeth looked yellow and coarse, as if made from horse hair, I couldn't be sure. It didn't look as if it had been made by Colgate, but it was a toothbrush. Yay!

"Zoe, I can't thank you enough," I said.

"The toothbrush was nothing, really," she smiled back.

"I didn't mean that," I replied.

"What then?"

"For talking."

"It's okay," she half-smiled at me. Then she paused as if to say something else.

"What?" I asked, cocking an eyebrow.

"Just be careful of Harry," she whispered, as if warning me somehow.

Before I'd had the chance to ask her what she meant, Zoe had gone, leaving me alone in my berth with bacon and eggs, a toothbrush, and my sore head.

25

After bathing in the porcelain tub in the bathroom along the corridor, I brushed my teeth, which felt good, and dressed in my cowgirl clothing. With the guns strapped against my thighs, I left the train. It was dusk and the sun was a mere semi-circle peeking over the tips of the Sangre de Cristo Mountains in the distance. The preacher had been right. As the dying sun cast its long red shadows over the tips of the mountains, it did look like a fountain of blood was flowing over them. I drew in a sharp breath as I studied their beauty in wonder. The white, snow-flecked peaks glistened with a crimson tinge and the mountains themselves looked almost mauve in colour. Deep gorges appeared like black shadows as the sun sank behind them like a fading star.

"Beautiful, aren't they?" someone said, and I turned to find the preacher standing beside me, a cigarette jutting out from beneath his droopy white moustache.

"Breath-taking," I murmured, looking back at the mountains.

"It's a cryin' shame the same can't be said about the creatures that lurk among them," he said, handing me a cigarette. I took it from him, and he held a match to it for me.

"Do you really believe there are vampires up there?" I asked.

"I don't just believe it," he said, blowing smoke from the corner of his mouth, his clear blue eyes staring at the mountains in the distance. "I know it."

I quietly smoked my cigarette and watched the preacher from the corner of my eye. He must have known I was looking at him, as he said, "It will be dark soon; come with us into town so you can get supplies."

"What kind of supplies?" I asked him.

"Bullets," he said, grinding out his cigarette in the dust with the heel of his boot. "You're gonna need as many as you can carry."

"Do bullets kill vampires?" I asked him.

"If you shoot them in the head enough times, it does." Then he was gone, striding along the platform.

I watched him go, cigarette smoke lingering around my fingers. I could see that Zoe, Louise, and Harry were waiting for him at the entrance to the station. Flicking the butt of the cigarette away with my thumb and fore-finger, I put my hat on and made my way towards them. Steam hissed in short bursts from the pistons attached to the *Scorpion Steam*'s wheels. Coal was being dropped into the tender behind the driver's cab from a contrap-tion which hung in the air above it. Clouds of black soot showered up into the red evening sky.

I reached the others, and trying hard not to make eye contact with Harry, I looked straight at Louise.

"Hi," I said.

"How are ya doing?" Louise asked with a smile.

"She's got a sore head," Zoe cut in with a giggle.

"Too much whiskey, I guess," I said, and shot a sideways glance at Harry, who just stared back at me.

"You were as drunk as a fiddler's clerk the last time I saw you," he said, with that grim-looking smile of his.

"Really?" I shot back at him with a snide look, wishing that we were alone so I could ask what, if anything, happened between us the night before. It was killing me not knowing for sure.

"Really," he said, and turned away.

Wanting to change the subject, and blushing like hell, I faced the preacher and said, "Where's Drake and his doctor friend?"

"Haven't seen them," the preacher said. "Still in bed, I reckon."

"If you hadn't had done that thing with the holy water last night, Sammy, I would have started to believe that Drake and the doctor were both a couple of bloodsuckers," Louise said.

Then, remembering the stunt I had pulled last night, I clapped my hand to my face, and looking at them, I said, "I'm really sorry about that last night. I didn't mean to . . . "

"You did nothing wrong," the preacher told me. "Someone had to find out if we were amongst vampires. I liked your thinking."

"But you seemed angry," I reminded him.

"Not at you," he grunted. Then looking at each of us, he added, "Let's get moving. We need to be back before dark."

Leading us through the small waiting room area, we stepped out onto a wide, dusty track which led straight into town. I could see the buildings a short walk away. The town was framed by the mountains in the distance. As we reached the main street, I saw a sign which read *Welcome to Silent Rest*.

I noticed at once that this town was different from Black Water Gap. Whereas that town had been bustling with life and noise, *Silent Rest* was just like its name – *silent*. The main street, which cut through the heart of the town, was deserted. Unlike the saloon we had stayed in, the bar in this town was closed for business. Tumbleweed blew lazily across the street in the chilly wind, which came down off the mountains. Even the Marshal's Office looked closed for business.

"Where is everyone?" Zoe asked the preacher, as the five of us walked side-by-side up the main street.

"In church, praying," the preacher said back, pointing towards a tall, white building at the end of the street.

Just like the church in Black Water Gap, it had a tall, white spire, which towered upwards. At the very top of this there was a brass bell. The roof of the church slanted away in both directions, and there was a wooden porch. On either side of this, there were two white-framed windows. Through them, I could see the orange glow of candlelight.

We reached the porch, and before pushing open its large double doors, the preacher looked back at us and said, "Take off your hats and show some respect – you're about to enter the Lord's house."

I removed my hat, letting it hang down against my back by its strap, and followed the others inside. There was a man standing before the congregation, who had all packed themselves into the church. Those who hadn't been able to find a seat stood in the aisles and gathered in a throng at the back of the church. The man at the front had been either talking or praying before the towns-people, but hearing us enter, he stopped and looked at us. Those whose heads weren't bowed in prayer turned to see what or who had disturbed their meeting. With their faces turned towards us, I could see fear in their eyes.

189

"So it's true," the man said, who stood before the others and pointed in our direction. "The Dark Man has arrived." He then made the sign of the cross over his chest and glanced up at the huge crucifix attached to the wall behind him. Then facing the congregation, he shouted, "We've been waiting for you, Preacher Man."

With his clear blue eyes keen and sharp, the preacher said, "I thought you called me a man of darkness – not of light."

"Darkness follows you, Preacher," the man said, and a tide of whispers passed amongst those packed into the church. "We were told that you were taking a train up into the mountains. News came from Black Water Gap that you left Hell behind you."

"You must forgive me," the preacher said back, "but I do not remember doing so."

I looked sideways at Harry, and his fingers hovered over his pistols.

"They found a woman," the man said. "She was slain, ripped to pieces. Her guts and her heart missing. Vampire's work, they say."

To hear the man speak reminded me of the article I'd read in the newspaper, but that murder had taken place in a town called Crows Ranch.

Had there been another committed right under our very noses in Black Water Gap? I wondered.

"Who says this about me?" the preacher asked, and

I saw Louise and Zoe hook their thumbs into their belts, their hands in reach of their guns.

"The Marshal and our preacher," the man said back, and I noticed several of the congregation cross themselves.

"And where are these men now?" the preacher called out as he looked about those huddled together in the candlelight.

"They went to intercept your train last night so you couldn't reach this place," he said as he stood in his dusty overalls. "But the fact that you're standing before us now, tells me that they failed in their mission."

Another wave of whispers passed over the crowd.

"The moment your train arrived in town, we gathered here knowing we would be protected in the Lord's house. He has offered sanctuary – but sadly, not to all of us."

"Who did the Lord fail to protect?" the preacher asked him, his eyes narrowing.

"The Marshal's wife," the man said. "Within minutes of your *Scorpion Steamer* arriving, her decapitated and disembowelled body was found behind the undertaker's. I've never seen such a thing. Looked as if she had been torn to pieces by the very devil himself. Just left lying there, she was, like a discarded lump of meat."

Again, I saw several members of the congregation cross themselves and murmur a prayer.

"So we gathered here and waited for sunset, knowing that's when you would come from that train. What they

191

say about you is true, Preacher," the man said. "Darkness does follow you."

Before the preacher had a chance to make any kind of response, the bell in the tower above us started to ring. Hearing its solemn boom, those gathered in the church began to shriek and cry hysterically.

"They're coming," the self-appointed leader of the town shouted. "Prove that you are still a man of light, Preacher, and protect us."

The preacher glanced sideways at us and nodded. He then left the church.

Not knowing what was about to happen, I followed the others out of the church. No sooner had the door closed behind me when I heard the sound of bolts being slid into place on the other side. Night had fallen while in the church, and moonlight blazed from behind a bank of cloud, which lumbered across the sky.

I looked down the length of Main Street, and could see the outline of the *Scorpion Steam* waiting at the platform. Black smoke poured from its funnel. I followed the others into the street. The bell stopped ringing from above and was replaced with the sound of horses galloping in our direction. I spun around and could see plumes of dust rising up from the foot of the mountains behind us.

"We've got company," the preacher breathed. Then looking at Harry, he said, "Go and get what we came for."

Harry nodded back at the preacher and raced down the centre of Main Street.

"C'mon," the preacher snapped at us, and headed after Harry.

I watched Harry stop outside the gunsmith's. He then ran at the door, colliding into it with his shoulder. The door blew inwards in a shower of splinters, as if being taken apart with a pile of explosives. Harry returned moments later, his arms crammed full with boxes of bullets. He hurriedly shared the boxes between us, and I filled my coat pockets with them.

Then, standing in the middle of Main Street facing the church, the preacher lit one of his smokes and said, "You all know what to do."

I wasn't sure that I did know what to do, but for the first time since arriving in 1888, I felt a sense of belonging. I felt a part of this team. The sound of hooves thundering over the hard-packed ground grew louder as a group of what looked like ten cowboys rode into town from behind the church. Seeing us spread across the street in a line, one of them raised a hand and the others brought their horses to a slow trot. They approached us, and as they did, I noticed that these cowboys had red bandanas pulled up over the lower part of their faces. All I could see were their eyes staring out from beneath their hats.

Although my heart was thumping inside my chest, that part of me, which now raced to the fore every time

I was in the shit, was scanning the outlaws who now came towards us. My mind was working out which one to kill first. When they were about ten feet away, they stopped and the outlaws sat and looked down at us. All I could see were their eyes shining brightly over the tops of the bandanas. Then, something happened that I could never have readied myself for.

26

The outlaws, if that's what they were, pulled down their bandanas and what I saw made me take a step backward. I immediately felt Harry's hand shove me forward again.

"Hold the line," he hissed.

I didn't look at Harry, as I couldn't take my eyes off the mouths of the outlaws. They were huge and crammed full of spiked teeth. Their mouths seemed to start just behind their ears, and join in what looked like an open wound in the front of their faces. Black blood dribbled from their fleshy grey gums and covered their chins. Their razor-sharp teeth glistened wetly in the dark.

"What the fuck are they?" I breathed.

"Oh, they're the Vrykolakas," Louise said matter-of-factly.

"Vampires?" I whispered, pushing pictures of Robert Pattinson from my mind.

"You bet," Harry said.

"Really?" I asked, glancing at him.

"You sound disappointed," he replied, not taking his eyes off the riders.

"It's just that I thought vampires were meant to be kinda sexy," I said. "These guys are like, really gross."

"Like I said," Harry groaned. "Sitting on your ass, thinking about cock all day long."

"Now, hold on a minute . . . " I started, but before I'd the chance to finish, all hell had broken loose.

No sooner had the first gun been fired, my own guns were in my fists and thundering. The vampires charged at us, their horses rearing up their front legs and kicking wildly. The vampires drew their guns and unleashed a volley of bullets. The preacher was out front, his right arm stretched out as his left hand snapped back and forth in a blinding flash over the hammer of his gun. Flashes of bright white light sparked from the end of his revolver as he fired with blinding speed at the vampires. I moved forward, my own guns almost seeming to explode in my fists as my fingers pulled repeatedly on the triggers. One of the vampires charged at me on his horse, his gun blazing smoke and fire. I dropped to the ground before the creature's giant hooves had a chance to trample me. Then I was up again, emptying my gun into the back of the vampire's head.

It exploded on his shoulders in a spray of red and grey mess. Although the vampire's body seemed to slope to one side, the horse kept running and running. I glanced at Harry, who was racing towards the charging vampires and not away from them. With his arms out front and aiming high, his mouth just a grim slit, he fired over and over again as he dodged the vampire's gunfire. He sunk a series of bullets into the chest of one of the creatures who flew back off his horse and into the air. Gripping the horse's reins, Harry raced alongside the fleeing horse and swung up into the saddle. He turned the horse and raced back towards the vampire who was now getting back up off the ground. It made a screeching noise in the back of its throat as it raced towards Harry, blood spraying in a red stream from its teeth. The vampire launched itself into the air, and for a moment, I thought Harry had been knocked from the horse. But as it raced past me, I saw that Harry had dropped backwards over the side of the horse. With one leg hooked over the saddle, he fired upwards into the vampire as he dropped out of the night at him.

With his guns blasting in his fists, the upper left side of the vampire's head blew away like a bloody Frisbee. The vampire dropped out of the sky like a stone and hit the ground, sending up a wake of dust. Hearing screaming behind me, I turned around to see a vampire launching himself out of his saddle at me. Its foaming mouth sprayed a jet of black blood into the air, but before its pointed teeth reached me, half of its jawbone was spinning away.

I glanced right and saw Louise firing wildly at it. The flashes from her gun lit up her eyes like fireworks. "I've got your back," she smiled at me. Then she spun around on the heel of her boots and emptied the rest of her bullets into the same vampire which raced towards her, half of its face missing. From the corner of my eye, I saw the preacher drop, and at first I thought he was injured. But when I looked again, I could see he was resting on one knee as he fired over and over again at the vampires which circled us on their giant black horses. Just like the barrels of his guns, the preacher's eyes seemed to be blazing, and in the darkness I was sure I could see him laughing. I saw Zoe come racing out of the shadows behind him, and it was then I realised why he had dropped onto one knee. With her guns in her hands, and a look of wild anger on her face, she ran up the length of the preacher's back. Timed with utter perfection, the preacher stood as her feet touched his shoulders, propelling her up. I watched in awe as Zoe spun and twisted through the air, her guns blazing. The vampires looked up in bewilderment as bullets rained down upon them. And while they looked up to see how they were being attacked from above, the rest of us seized the moment and filled their upturned faces with lead.

The sound of gunfire was deafening, and the smell of gunpowder intoxicating in some strange way. I watched Zoe spiral out of the air and land in the saddle behind one of the vampires. Before he'd a chance to even look back, Zoe had placed her guns on either side of his head and pulled both triggers. The last of the vampires' heads exploded or imploded, it happened so quickly I couldn't be sure. All I could see was a fountain of red shower up into the night.

Zoe threw the vampire's corpse from the horse and raced towards the preacher. Hanging from the side of the horse, she dropped her arm. The preacher grabbed it, swung up into the air, landing into the saddle in front of her. Then, before I knew what was happening, I was being lifted off my feet and thrown backwards. I landed in the saddle facing Harry as he raced after the preacher. I looked left and could see Louise racing alongside us. Her long black hair whipped back off her face and her eyes shone with excitement, bordering on lust.

At the end of Main Street, the preacher slowed his horse and brought it to a stop and we joined him. Gathered together, we looked back at the church and the pile of vampire bodies we had left behind.

"That wasn't so bad," Harry remarked.

I was pressed against his chest. His shirt was open and I could see a thin line of sweat run down his neck and across his smooth hard skin.

No sooner had the words left his mouth when the sound of rumbling filled the air, and another posse of vampires rode into the street from just behind the church.

"Okay, maybe not so easy," he muttered, yanking on the reins.

"And they're not our only problem," the preacher hissed. "That son-of-a-bitch Drake is leaving without us."

At once, we all glanced around to see the *Scorpion Steam* chugging out of the station.

27

"Drake's sold us out," Louise spat, prodding the sides of the horse with her calves and galloping off after the fast-disappearing train.

"We need to get back on board," the preacher shouted over the sound of the approaching vampires. "We can't stay out here!" Then he was gone, racing away with Zoe in pursuit of his lover and the train.

Harry made a loud clucking noise in the back of his throat and pulled me closer against him as we galloped away. I glanced back over his shoulder and could see the vampires racing after us. I counted ten of them, their bandanas dropped and fangs exposed. Placing my hands on Harry's shoulders, I tried to position myself in the saddle, so I had a clear shot over his shoulder.

"What are you doing?" he roared back at me.

"You just keep your eyes on that train and leave everything else to me," I shouted. I gripped his muscular shoulder with my left hand to keep myself steady, and pressing myself flat against him, I drew my gun. As I levered myself into position and to keep a grip of him, I wrapped my legs around his waist. As I rode up against him, I felt my breasts brush against his face.

He made a mumbling noise against me.

"Say what?" I shouted. "Stop mumbling!"

"Get your tits outter my face!" he roared at me. "I can't see a god-damn thing!"

"Oh stop getting so excited!" I shouted back at him. "It was an accident for crying out loud"

He made a grunting noise in the back of his throat.

Rocking back and forth in the saddle as Harry raced the horse forwards, I took aim at the vampires, who were nearly upon us, and fired. The lead vampire's head flew back off its shoulders. The horse raced on as if carrying the Headless Horseman from *The Legend of Sleepy Hollow*. I fired again, but my gun just clicked dry.

Reaching down with my other hand, I tried to free one of Harry's guns from around his waist.

"Now's not the time," he snapped back, knocking my hand away from his groin.

"I'm not reaching for your cock, you moron," I yelled over the sound of the shrieking vampires who were now within touching distance of us. "I need your gun!"

202

Slinging it from his holster, he handed it to me. I snatched it out of his hand. It was heavier and bigger than mine. I pulled the trigger with lightning speed, aiming the gun at the vampires' heads. Bullet after bullet thudded into the faces of the vampires, but it took more than just one bullet to kill them. The vampires returned fire as they raced alongside us, their horses looking unnaturally huge and powerful. They were black and sleek-looking, like the one Harry and I rode.

One of the vampires reached for me with a white hooked claw. Its yellow fingernails slashed through the leg of my denims, cutting it into fine shreds. I lurched backwards and Harry placed one of his hands on my arse to steady me. I glanced at him.

"Don't go getting any funny ideas, doll," he snapped back at me.

Harry drove the horse harder. The vampire drew level with us and lunged for me again, its face just inches from mine. The creature was so close I could see that just beneath its pale skin there was a mass of blue and mauve veins, which seemed to wriggle like worms hatching in its flesh. The vampire's eyes were dead black, and I could see my own reflection in them. But it was its mouth which was the most horrific thing about its features. It was so open and wide that its jagged lips seemed to ripple in the rushing wind. They made a flapping noise and the vampire's breath smelt of decaying meat. Its tongue was swollen and purple and the tip ran over a set of gums which wept black blood and white puss. This close up to the creature's teeth, they looked like knives, each one of them jagged and broken and razor-sharp.

With my guns dry and needing to keep hold of Harry, I rolled my free fist back, and punched the vampire straight in the face. It looked at me with surprise, like that was the last thing it had expected me to do.

"That's how girls where I come from deal with arse-holes!" I shouted, then glanced at Harry.

The vampire's skin felt spongy and some of it fell away, black and rotten-looking from around the spot where my fist had connected with its face. Glancing back over Harry's shoulder, I could see we were galloping alongside the *Scorpion Steam*. Gunfire was being sprayed from the sky, and I looked up to see Louise charging along the roof of the train, her long black hair and coat-tails flowing out behind her. Then I saw Zoe leap from the horse which she had been riding with the preacher. She clung to the side of the speeding train, racing up a metal ladder which was attached to the side of the carriage. Placing one hand over the other, she raced with speed up onto the roof, where she joined Louise in picking off the vampires with the bullets they pumped from their revolvers.

I watched as one vampire after another flew back into the air, blood spraying from the holes in their necks where their hideous heads had moments before been attached.

"Go! Go! Go!" Harry suddenly roared at me as we drew level with the carriage. Holding him tight, I tried to climb out of the saddle. Again I brushed against him. I reached for the side of the speeding train, then glanced back at Harry. He looked at me. A few remaining vampires raced just behind him, and I could see they were preparing themselves to jump onto the train. Then dropping back into the saddle and placing my cheek next to his, I whispered in his ear, "If we're gonna die, I just want to know one thing."

"What's that!" he whispered back, his breath warm against my face, and making the hairs at the base of my neck prickle.

"Did we make love last night?" I breathed over the sound of gunfire and screaming vampires. I know I hadn't picked the best of times to ask, but I needed to know, just in case one of us didn't make it.

"No," he said his stubble rubbing against my cheek.

"You're a liar," I whispered, our lips just inches apart.

Then, staring into my eyes, Harry said, "We didn't make love, we had sex. There is a difference, you know."

"You are such an arrogant, self-conceited, chauvinistic, half-brained dickhead!" I spat at him, clambering out of the saddle. I didn't want him to touch me. Not ever.

"I don't understand what half of that meant. But now's not the time to become hysterical," he shouted back at me.

"I'm not *hysterical*!" I screeched at him, bullets whizzing overhead. "I just can't believe I let someone like you sleep with me!"

"You weren't doing a lot of sleeping, as far as I can remember," he yelled back. "Now if I were you, I'd get on board that damn train before you get us both killed!"

"I'd quite like to see you killed," I hissed under my breath and threw myself at the train.

"Nice!" he shouted back, just to let me know he had heard what I'd muttered.

Ignoring him, I scrambled up the ladder. The preacher was now standing alongside the others and all three of them were firing down at the last of the vampires who chased after Harry. With a fluidity that I was unaware I had, I reloaded the gun with the bullets from my pockets in seconds, and joined in firing at the vampires. I watched Harry stand up in the stirrups, and letting go of the reins, he threw himself at the side of the train. At the same time, the last of the vampires flung itself from its horse. But unlike Harry, it didn't need a ladder; it used its long claws to scurry along the side of the carriage. Harry saw it but was too late. The vampire gripped hold of Harry's leg and threw its head back, as if to sink its teeth into him.

Then, the vampire's head was hanging open, its brains streaming out of its fractured skull as the train raced up the mountainside.

"Great shot!" Louise said, twirling her guns in her hands and then sliding them into their holsters.

The preacher reached down and yanked Harry up onto the roof of the train, then suddenly he collapsed; they all did, except Louise.

The preacher, Harry, and Zoe dropped to their knees and gripped their stomachs. Each one cried out, as if in agony.

"*Stop the train!*" the preacher roared, his face white and streaming sweat.

"Stop the train?" I gasped, looking down into his tortured face. "But the vampires!"

"They're dead," Louise screeched, wrapping her arm around the preacher's shoulders.

"But more might come," I said, looking down at Harry who was now lying on his side and howling in pain.

"They hunt in packs," Louise snapped at me, as if this was something I should have known. "They won't come back tonight; besides we're far away from Silent Rest."

I looked at Zoe, who was now convulsing on the roof of the train, her tongue lolling from the corner of her mouth.

"What's wrong with them?" I gasped, not understanding what was happening.

"*Stop the train!*" Louise yelled at me, her own eyes now brimming with fear. "We have to get them off the train or we're all gonna die!"

I stumbled backwards as I made my way along the

roof of the train. I reached the end of the carriage and scrambled down the ladder and into the carriage. I raced into the passageway, and seeing the emergency stop chain, I pulled on it with all my strength. There was a deafening hissing sound as the brakes locked on and the train began to slow. The carriage lurched violently and I stumbled onto the floor. I pulled myself up and ran back down the passageway. By the time I reached the ladder again, the train had stopped. I climbed it and hoisted myself back onto the roof. With thick black smoke curling all around me from the funnel, I covered my eyes with my arms and ran back to where the preacher and the others had collapsed. The smoke was so thick that it was almost impossible to see anything. Then the clouds broke above me and milky-blue moonlight lit up the roof. I looked front and back and couldn't see my friends anywhere. It was like they had vanished.

28

"What's going on?" I heard someone shout from below, their feet crunching over the ballast.

I looked over the edge of the train and could see the light from an oil lamp swinging in the dark.

"Who's there?" I called out, my guns in my fists.

"It's Doctor Dable," the voice shouted. "Now what on earth is going on?"

I holstered my guns and climbed back down the ladder attached to the side of the carriage. I landed trackside and peered into the darkness. The doctor stepped from the gloom, his face like a Halloween mask in the orange glow from the lamp. His eyes were black and did nothing to reflect the lamplight. His face was pale, gaunt, and tired-looking.

"They've gone," I said, peering into the darkness, looking for any sign of my friends.

"Who has?" the doctor snapped. "What are you talking about, child?"

"The preacher and the others," I told him.

"And their horses, too," Drake said, stepping from the darkness and standing next to his doctor. He looked tired too, but his eyes looked alive and excited somehow. His lips were a crimson line beneath his nose.

"What do you mean the horses have gone? That's impossible!" I breathed, not knowing or understanding what had happened to the others. The last time I had seen them was only moments ago, and apart from Louise, they had been rolling around in agony.

"See for yourself," Drake said, pointing down the length of the train. "The carriage door has been dropped and the horses have gone."

I hurried along the cess, which rang alongside the tracks. The ballast crunched under my boots, and the light from the doctor's lamp lit my way. I reached the carriage where the horses had been stabled and could see that all of them had been taken, except for mine.

"They've gone, ratted out on us," Drake said with a sneer. "Call themselves vampire hunters? The first sign of trouble and they disappear."

Wheeling around, I glared at Drake and said, "As far as I can remember, it was you who did the disappearing act. You left without us. We could've been killed back there thanks to you!"

"I didn't pay the preacher and his band of merry men and women for their company," Drake said. "I paid them to protect me and that's what they were doing while I made good on my escape."

"Aww, you're such a hero," I sneered at him.

Turning from me, he looked at his companion and said, "Doctor, speak to the driver and tell him to get this train rolling again."

"What!" I spat. "You can't just leave without them."

"They've already gone," Drake hissed at me. "I'm not prepared to wait around here in the middle of nowhere in the dead of night. It's too dangerous."

"They'll be back," I tried to convince him.

"Nonsense. They've gone, fled into the night. They've taken their horses. They won't be back. Now you can come with us, or take your chances out here in the wilderness." Then, looking at the doctor again, he snapped, "Why are you still standing here? Tell the driver to get this train going again."

With my hand seizing my gun with frightening speed, I pointed it at the both of them and said, "We're not going anywhere. They went away before and came back. They'll do the same again."

Drake and the doctor eyed the barrel of my gun. Then moving slowly towards me with the aid of his walking stick, Drake placed his hand over the end of my gun and slowly lowered it. "You say that the preacher and his gang disappeared before? When was this, please tell me?"

"The night we stayed at the saloon in Black Water . . . "

Before I'd the chance to finish, Drake turned to the doctor and said, "Tell the driver to hold the train. I think Miss Carter and I need to have a little chat."

Glad to hear that the train wouldn't be leaving until my friends returned, I looked at Drake and said, "So what do you want to talk about?"

"The preacher, of course," he smiled back at me, and then made his way back onto the train.

I followed him to the observation carriage, where he dropped into one of the comfortable-looking armchairs beneath the glass roof. Drake crossed one leg over the next at the ankles and lit himself a cigarette. With smoke curling from the corner of his mouth, he passed me the silver cigarette case and book of matches. I took one, lit it, and then sat in the chair opposite him. The doctor joined us and stood just behind Drake and looked at me. I felt as if I was going to be interrogated somehow. I'd never been arrested by the police and interviewed, but I wondered if it wouldn't have felt very much like this.

Without taking his eyes off me, Drake reached into the breast pocket of his dark grey suit, removed what looked like a small black leather wallet, and threw it onto the table before us.

"What's that?" I asked him.

"Take a look for yourself," he smiled at me again, and took a long, slow puff on his cigarette.

I picked up the leather wallet and opened it. At first I thought I was imagining what I was seeing. On one side there was a silver badge about the size of a large coin. On the other side there was a white business card which read, *Detective Sergeant Drake, Scotland Yard.*

"Get outta here," I sighed in disbelief. "You're no copper."

What part of my unconscious mind had created this? I wondered.

"I am indeed," he said. Then motioning towards the doctor he said, "And my companion, the good doctor, is a police surgeon. Both of us are employed by Scotland Yard."

The doctor nodded at me, as if this was the first time we had officially been introduced.

I blew smoke from the corner of my mouth, and throwing the warrant card back onto the table, I said, "So if you really are who you say you are, what are you doing so far from home?"

"We're tracking a killer, Miss Carter," and his eyes beamed with excitement.

"What killer?" I said, still trying to play catch-up.

"Jack the Ripper," he said, sitting forward in his chair and rubbing his hands together.

"So if you really are hunting the Ripper," I asked

him, "what's the deal with the train and the whole, 'I'm a rich gent who wants to do a bit of gold mining' thing?"

"We needed a cover story," Drake started to explain. "We needed to get into the mountains – and fast, before the trail went cold." Then, with a solemn look on his face, he added, "Like you, Miss Carter, my companion and I believe the Ripper to be a vampire."

"I never said I believed Jack the Ripper to be a vampire," I shot back.

"You say you don't," he said snuggly, "but in your heart, you do believe him to be so. You said as much last night at dinner."

"I did not," I said.

"I asked you directly last night, before leaving the dining car, if you believed Jack the Ripper was a vampire and you said . . . " and taking a notebook from his pocket, he flipped it open and read from it. "And you said, Miss Carter, 'I don't know what to believe anymore.'"

"Jesus, this really is like a police interview," I whispered.

"That's because we are the police," he smiled, placing the notebook back into his pocket. "Admit it, you know the Ripper is a vampire. You said yourself you were hunting him. You chased him down onto that train as he fled the murder of his last victim, Mary Jane Kelly. He strangled you, rendered you defenceless, and somehow brought you here."

"But . . . " I started, wanting to tell him that I wasn't chasing Jack the Ripper who preyed on the women of Whitechapel in 1888, but I was trying to prove the existence of a vampire in 2012.

"But what?" Drake cut over me. "You woke up just outside the town of Black Water Gap and who was waiting for you? The preacher. Who is this man that claims to be holy? I've never known such a man. He claims to hunt vampires – he *is* a vampire!"

"I just saw him kill about twenty tonight," I said, trying to defend the preacher.

"A mere smokescreen," Drake snapped. "To throw us off his scent. Look at the facts, Miss Carter. You said yourself that there had just recently been a Ripper-style murder in the town of Crows Ranch, which I hasten to add that you have to pass through to get to Black Water Gap . . . "

"Stop," I said almost falling from my seat. "There was a murder in Black Water Gap, too."

"How do you know this?" the doctor asked, coming around from behind Drake's chair and standing beside it.

"A man from the town of Silent Rest told us," I whispered, a terrible sinking feeling in my heart. Then looking at both of them, I added, "There was another murder there, too."

"When?" Drake said, leaping from his seat and rubbing his hands together.

"Just after the train arrived in town today," I answered, a part of me hating every word that I said as it pointed the finger of blame at the preacher.

"And the victim?" the doctor asked me.

"Female," I breathed. "She had her throat slit and intestines removed, just like the others."

"Just like the victims back home in London," Drake said, looking at me and the doctor. Then rushing across the carriage towards me, an excitable glint in his eyes, he said, "You said that the preacher disappeared that night back in Black Water Gap?"

"Yes," I nodded.

"Would that have been the very same night the woman would have been murdered?"

"Yes," I nodded again, trying to comprehend what I was learning. "But what about the others, Harry, Zoe, and Louise?"

"Accomplices!" Drake said, as if he had finally put the last pieces of the jigsaw together.

Then, feeling the blood draining from my face, I remembered watching Louise as she washed blood from her hands in the drinking trough outside the saloon.

"What's wrong, child?" the doctor asked, taking up my wrist and searching for a pulse with his fingers. "You look as if you're going to faint."

"Pour her some whiskey," Drake barked.

"No," I said, shaking my head. "No more whiskey."

"What is wrong then?" the doctor asked me again. "You look as if you have just seen a ghost."

"I saw blood on her hands," I breathed, looking at Drake and the doctor.

"Whose hands?" Drake asked, leaning over me.

"Louise's hands," I told him. "The night they disappeared, I saw her on her return, washing blood from her hands."

"Accomplices," Drake said again, as if hammering home the point and trying to prove he had been right all along. "She cleans up after him, washes away the evidence."

"And the others?" I asked, hoping that perhaps there was a hole in his theory. Because if there wasn't, I had been wronged; tricked and deceived by the people I had come to think of as my friends.

"Don't you see what is plainly looking you straight in the face, Miss Carter?" Drake asked. "All of them are vampires."

I thought of how I'd seen Harry race along the riverbank at an incredible speed, how he had slaughtered that bear with his hands – or had they been claws? I shuddered inwardly as I remembered how his hands and voice had seemed different while making love – sorry – *having sex* with me.

"But the holy water, the mirrors?" I said, my mind scrambling to find gaps in his belief that all of them were vampires.

"Myths and legends," Drake snapped. "Stories which

have been created over the centuries. Where is the proof that vampires are doomed by mere trinkets and water?"

As I tried to think of another reason why my friends couldn't possibly be vampires, my heart sank again as I remembered what the vampire had said to me on the Tube train as I'd splashed him with holy water.

Holy water doesn't work, nor does the garlic I can smell in your pocket, or the crucifix which glistens between your breasts, he had whispered in my ear.

Feeling sick, I looked at Drake and said, "So if what you say is true about the preacher and the others, what are you going to do?"

"I'll tell you what *we* are going to do," Drake said. "*We're* going to pretend that we know nothing of what or who they really are."

"But they must be stopped," I said, getting up from my seat.

"And they will be!" Drake exclaimed. "I already have wheels in motion to stop this vicious gang in their very tracks. But if we reveal our hand too soon – they will slaughter us in our beds. Make no mistake about that, Miss Carter."

"What do you have planned?" I asked him.

"We're heading for The Hanging Mine," Drake explained, lighting himself another smoke. "We should arrive there tomorrow at nightfall. We will be met there by the full force of the law."

"How will they know to meet us there?" I asked.

"They were dispatched the very moment we left Black Water Gap," he smiled knowingly.

"Those men in the bowler hats were police officers," I said.

"Exactly," and his eyes twinkled again.

"And should we need a real holy man to bless some water, the preacher from the town of Silent Rest is already en route. He travels with the town's marshal for protection."

Remembering what I had learnt from the town of Silent Rest, I said, "It was the marshal's wife who was slain by the . . . " I couldn't finish.

"The preacher?" Drake asked cocking an eyebrow at me.

I nodded.

"Oh dear," he said. "This just gets worse and worse."

"I think the marshal will welcome the opportunity of coming face to face with the preacher – the man who we will discover has killed his wife," the doctor said.

I stood silently for a moment, my mind racing as I tried to comprehend everything I had learnt.

"Do you think you will be unable to continue with your pretence until we reach the mine tomorrow night, Miss Carter?" Drake asked, watching me.

"What pretence?"

"That you are friends with these . . . vampires," he said.

"Do I have a choice?" I asked, eyeing him.

"Of course you do," Drake smiled grimly. "One will lead to snaring a vicious killer, and the other, your own death."

Without saying another word, I crossed the carriage, heading for the door. I just wanted to lock myself away in my room until this trip was over. A part of me now prayed that my friends didn't come back. One, because they were walking into a trap that I was helping to lay, and the other . . . they were killers. I pulled open the carriage door and Drake spoke from behind me.

"Remember, Miss Carter, not a word. All of our lives depend upon it," he said.

I turned my back on him and left the carriage.

29

I don't know how long I'd been talking to Drake and the doctor for, but as I passed down the narrow connecting passageways, the first rays of the morning winter sun shone in through the windows. As I made my way back to my carriage with my head spinning, I tried desperately to understand everything that Drake had told me. He seemed to have everything figured out. He had an answer for everything. But I had one question, which I knew he wouldn't be able to answer.

What was I doing back in 1888, chasing down Jack the Ripper? I wondered.

I reached my carriage feeling physically and emotionally exhausted. I was tired, but I doubted I would sleep. I had too much going around and around in my mind. My room was dark, the curtains pulled across the windows. Then, the door slammed shut behind me, and someone wrapped their arm about my throat.

I gasped, and a hand fell across my mouth.

"Shhh," the person whispered in my ear.

Someone lit a match, and the light from it glowed weakly. The match was held to one of the oil lamps, and the flame was turned down, just casting enough light so I could barely make out the silhouette of two people seated in the armchairs. Their outlines were big enough to tell me that both were men. Whoever it was who had lit the lamp passed across the room like a shadow and sat on the sofa. This shadowy figure was smaller in size.

The hand loosened from my mouth, as did the arm around my throat. I gripped the arm of whoever held me and I spun around to face them. I found myself looking into Louise's dark eyes. Holding her arm, I looked down at the bandage which still covered her wrist and yanked it free. Even in the pale light thrown by the lamp I could see that there wasn't any cut or injury like she had said there to be.

"Drake was right," I gasped.

"He was right about what?" the preacher's voice whispered from out of the darkness.

I spun around, and as my eyes gradually grew accustomed to the gloom, I could just make out that it was the preacher who sat in one of the armchairs. Fearing that I had said way too much already, I stood silently before him. I looked at the other black outlines and knew that they belonged to Harry and Zoe.

I heard the key twist in the lock behind me as Louise pushed me away from the door. I looked back and could see her standing with her back against it, barring my escape. Knowing that I had to keep Drake's secret, I ignored the preacher's question and asked one of my own.

"So where did you guys rush off to?"

"What did Drake say?" and this time it was Harry who asked the question, his voice floating out of the darkness as quiet as a whisper.

Instinctively I reached for my guns, but Louise was quicker than me, and had snatched them from their holsters.

"Sammy, you won't need your guns," the preacher said, and I wished that I could see him. "We're not going to hurt you."

"Turn the lamp up so I can see you," I breathed.

"You don't need to see us," the preacher sighed.

"Yes, I do," I said right back.

"Why?" he asked, his voice curious.

Then swallowing hard and guessing the preacher knew I had them all figured out, I said, "Drake says that you are a vampire. He says you all are."

"Does he now?" the preacher chuckled, and it sounded deep and rasping. "And what do you think, Sammy? What is it that you *believe*?"

"I don't know what to believe," I whispered.

"Where is your faith?" the preacher asked me softly.

"I don't think I have any," I replied honestly.

"Are you like the disciple Thomas?" he asked, as the others sat silently in the dark. "Do you need to see that we are not vampires before you really believe us?"

"Yes," I said.

"Very well."

Zoe's shadowy form reached out and picked up the lamp and passed it to the preacher. Slowly, he raised it before him and I threw my hands to my face in shock. His eyes were yellow and piercing with blood-red pupils. Although he still looked like his former self, thick white eyebrows curled up in points at his temples. His white moustache spread over his cheeks, giving him the appearance of having a straggly-looking beard. Hair hung from his chin in silver wispy lengths. The preacher's ears seemed longer somehow – pointed. But it was his skin; it looked dry and flaky, like scales which were reforming, growing together again. He had angry-looking boils on his forehead and cheeks. Wisps of hair jutted out of some of these, but others just wept black goo. His lips were swollen and covered in white blisters. He smiled at me, and his lips cracked open, showing raw flesh underneath. I could see the preacher had two long pointed teeth at each corner of his mouth. If he was a vampire, he looked nothing like the creatures that had attacked us the night before.

"What kind of creature are you?" I breathed, in shock.

"We have been called many things," the preacher said handing the light back to Zoe and disappearing into the dark again so I could no longer look upon his face. "Vargulfs, Wargs, Therianthrope, but my favourite is Turnskins," he said.

"What do those words mean?" I asked.

"They have lots of meanings, Sammy," he explained gently. "Vargulf means rogue, outlaw, or wolf. Wargs, the wearer of wolf skin. Therianthrope, means beast man . . . "

"And Turnskins?" I gasped, my heart now thumping as I realised what it was he was trying to tell me. "What is a Turnskin?"

"A hound of God," he whispered, his voice raw and dry. "Werewolves, dear Sammy, we're werewolves."

30

I raced across the darkened room to the door. I needed to get out – to tell Drake that there were werewolves on the train. Louise gripped my arm as I frantically twisted the door handle.

"I have the key and your guns, remember?" she whispered in my ear.

Wheeling around, I looked at her in the gloom and said, "So you're a wolf, too?"

"No," she said. "I'm very human."

"But you've been . . . you know . . . sleeping with the preacher," I said. Then, suddenly a thought hit me like a punch to the face and I gasped, "Oh, my God! I've made love to a werewolf!"

"We had sex," Harry said from the darkness, his voice deeper but dark and smooth sounding.

"Whatever it was, it wasn't normal – *natural!*" I cried.

"Thanks," Harry said back.

"I don't believe this is happening to me," I cried, slapping my temples with the flat of my hands. "C'mon, Sammy wake up! You can do it – just think of home. Think of that train and you'll wake up and those cops will come and save you!"

"Are you okay?" I heard someone ask, and it was Zoe's voice that I could hear.

"No, I'm not fucking okay!" I shouted at her black form. Then, pulling free of Louise's hold I raced across the room to the curtains. I gripped them and just as I was going to flood the carriage with light so I could see them, the preacher spoke up.

"I wouldn't do that if I were you."

"And give me one good reason why not," I snapped, my hands poised.

"Because you will kill us," Harry said, and I could feel him standing behind me. "We're not a danger to you now. We're in the final stages of changing back to our human form, but we need another hour or two of darkness. That's why the preacher looks like does – like we all do, because we were caught out in light before we had changed back. The sun could still kill us. You don't want that do you, Sammy?" and I felt his hand – claw – paw – whatever, gently squeeze my shoulder.

I let the curtains slide through my fingers, and shrugging his hand away from me, I stepped back from him.

"Thank you," he said, his outline huge and powerful-looking in the dark.

"I thought it was only vampires who couldn't go around in the sun?" I said, still feeling angry, confused, and hurt.

"Both creatures are just two different sides of the same dark coin," the preacher spoke up. "We are very similar. But there are differences."

"And what might they be?" I quipped. "Vampires like ripping the throats out of innocent people, and you howl at the moon and take a leak up a tree?"

"Something like that," the preacher said. "But I don't ever remember taking a leak against a tree. You're going to have to forget any preconceived ideas that you may or may not have about werewolves, Sammy."

"I don't have to do anything," I hissed at him.

"If you're going to tag along with our pack then you need to listen to the preacher," Zoe said softly. I wished that I could see her, but then again, did I really want to? If she looked anything like the preacher had, then I was pretty sure that I didn't want to see her.

"I'm not planning on hanging around with any pack," I snapped at her. "I just want to go home. Back to London. Back to twenty . . . "

"But we need you," Louise said from behind me. "We were hoping . . . I was hoping that you might help me."

"With what, exactly?" I said into the darkness.

"I watch the preacher, Harry, and Zoe while they are

wolves – take care of them, if you like. That's where you saw me returning from the other night in Black Water Gap. During a full moon, the preacher and the others fully change, become savage, just like wild wolves. So I keep them chained – locked up – so they can't harm anyone. It was the blood of a deer that you saw me wash from my hands that night. I kill for them when they are changed to satisfy their hunger and bloodlust."

"I still don't see how I can help you?" I said, still not truly believing what I was hearing.

"They can use their powers of speed, strength, and their appearance can even change a little at any time. But during a full moon, when they are fully transformed, they become cunning and will do and say anything to be free of the shackles they willingly put on before their change. But once wolves, they will tell you anything, plead with you, beg you, trick you into setting them free. Sometimes the full moon can last three or more nights, and to stay awake for so long can weaken my resolve. It is easy when you are so tired to become weak and believe the lies and the tricks they will tell you to be set free."

"If it's such a drain on you, why haven't you hired some help before?" I asked. "Although I'd love to read the role requirements for that job. I can only begin to imagine what the interview for the post would be like."

"There was another," the preacher said. "Her name was Marley Cooper."

I glanced down at Zoe, and although I could only see her rough outline in the dark, I said, "I remember you mentioning Marley, and Drake thought I was her when we first met in the saloon. Who was she?"

"She was my friend," Louise spoke up. "She watched the Skinturners through the long nights with me. We would sit together as they begged and pleaded to be released."

"So what happened to her?" I insisted.

There was silence in the darkness, and the only sound I could hear was my own heartbeat pounding in my chest.

"I killed her," Harry suddenly said, his voice calm.

"You killed her?" I gasped in disbelief, knowing that I had made love to him – *had sex* with him. I mustn't get that confused, or I might soon be dead.

"I had good reason," Harry said, his voice deep.

"What good reason could you possibly have for killing someone?" I snapped at him, feeling even more angry and confused than I had before.

"The same reasons you had for killing those five men and those vampires last night," he reminded me. "You did it for the same reason that I killed Marley – you did it to survive."

"What threat could a woman have been to a werewolf?" I seethed.

"She loved me . . . " he started.

"Oh well, there you go then!" I sighed. "God forbid

any woman who goes and falls in love with the great Harry Turner."

"Be quiet," he boomed. "You don't understand. I loved Marley Cooper – yes I was in love with her. But she wanted more than I was prepared to give."

"Don't tell me," I sneered, "She asked you to say the magic 'L' word?"

"She wanted me to bite her," Harry said. "She wanted me to change her – she wanted to be like us. Marley wanted to be a wolf. I tried to tell her it was a curse on one's soul. Being a Turnskin is a nightmare that I have to live with every day. I didn't want that for her. But Marley believed that if I truly loved her, then I would change her. So when I refused time and time again, she grew bitter and resentful. Unless I am beheaded, speared through the heart with a silver sword, or bitten by a vampire, then I am immortal – we all are. But she wanted the strength and the power that we have. She wanted to live for ever. But I didn't care for that. Marley believed that immortality was a gift – but it isn't. It's a curse, I tell you."

"If your life is such a nightmare, why didn't you just kill yourself instead of her?" I spat.

"We can't kill ourselves – not intentionally. And we can't kill each other, as we have all come from the same bite, the same bloodline," Harry explained, and the others sat quietly while he told his story. "So, Marley's love for me turned to mistrust, spite, and jealousy.

Unbeknown to us, she struck a deal with the vampires. In exchange for the location of where we would hide during our next change, knowing that we would be chained and defenceless, she would receive the immortality that she craved so much, from a vampire bite."

"How did you find out about this betrayal?" I asked him, moving slightly in the dark, trying to get a glimpse of him as a wolfman.

"That day, the day the preacher found you in the desert and brought you back to camp – you were unconscious. Zoe discovered Marley throwing away a crucifix, a bottle of holy water, and some cloves of garlic, which she had found in your coat pocket. Now why would she have wanted to get rid of the very articles that would protect us from our enemies? That night as you lay unconscious in the wagon, and we had been chained up, Louise saw the vampires coming across the plain," Harry explained. "We had been chained up for three nights, the moon going through a particularly slow cycle. For hours Louise had listened to our howling, begging, and empty promises, so she took a break and walked away from the camp. It was then she saw the vampires coming on their wild black horses. Louise rushed back and told Marley what she had seen. Marley told her what she had done, and that it was too late for me and the others, but not for her. Louise begged Marley for the keys to our chains so we could be released, even if it meant her own certain death.

"But Marley wouldn't hand over the keys, and told her to run and run and run. Unbeknown to Marley, I had overheard her and Louise's heated argument. So knowing that we had been tricked, I told Marley that if she unchained me, I would bite her – not kill her – just bite her so she could become like me. Believing that her prayers had been answered, she hurriedly unchained me . . . "

"And you killed her," I finished for him.

"Yes," he whispered. "Or spend the rest of my life sleeping with one eye open. I knew I could never trust her again."

"As I told you once before, Sammy, the Lord gives you what you need, not what you ask for," the preacher said.

"So Marley needed to die?" I shot back.

"She was dead either way," the preacher came back at me. "If Harry hadn't killed her – the vampires would of, then us, too."

"But the vampires promised to give her eternal life," I said.

"There is only one who can give that," the preacher whispered. "What the vampires offered Marley, and what she so wanted from Harry, isn't eternal life – it's a living hell. You are nothing more than the walking dead, feeding off the living, and damning your soul forever. She would have never been given eternal life if she had chosen that path."

"So what about the women you've been killing?" I said, looking at his dark shape slumped in the armchair. "You've been doing them a favour too, I guess?"

"What women?" the preacher asked me, his voice barely above a whisper.

"The women that Drake believes you have murdered."

"Why would he say something like that?" he asked, a dry chuckle in the back of his throat.

"Because he believes you're Jack the Ripper," I told him.

31

An eerie silence fell over the carriage, and apart from the sound of my own heart racing in my chest, all I could hear was the sound of the wind howling down off the mountains and buffeting the side of the train. Just as the silence became almost unbearable, the preacher spoke.

"Now why would Drake think that I was this Jack the Ripper? What does some rich mining tycoon know about me?"

"Well that's the real trick," I said, wondering how much I should tell him about what I had learnt from Drake. But in my heart I wanted to tell the preacher. However scared I felt at being in the presence of werewolves, none of them had hurt me. They'd all had plenty of opportunities to kill me or make me one of them, but they hadn't. So drawing a deep breath, I said, "Drake isn't a miner, he's a police officer. He works for Scotland Yard. The doctor who travels with him is a police surgeon, and together, they are hunting the Ripper."

"Who they happen to believe is me," the preacher said, and although I couldn't see his face, he sounded amused by this.

"Yes," I nodded, staring into the darkness at his outline. "There was a murder in a town called Crows–"

"Ranch," the preacher finished for me. "I also read the newspapers, Sammy. And as we also now know, there was another in Black Water Gap, and one shortly after we arrived in Silent Rest. I can see why this lawman might suspect me. I have recently been in all three locations. But I have three others who will provide me with an alibi."

I knew he was referring to Harry, Zoe, and Louise, so I said, "Drake thinks the others are your accomplices."

"They were chained up on the night of those murders," Louise said, coming to stand beside the table with the low-burning lamp on it.

Her pale, tired face looked haunted in the light. "But you weren't," I whispered.

"So you think I'm the killer now?" she sighed with frustration.

"No," I breathed shaking my head, "Unless, you've been to London lately."

"Ah, yes," the preacher said, "Isn't this Jack the Ripper the man you were chasing through London Town? The man that you told us strangled you and then you miraculously woke up here?"

"Yes," I said.

"Then unless I've grown a pair of wings and flown from one side of the world to the other, then it couldn't have been me or any one of us," the preacher said.

"Drake believes that it was you I was chasing, it was you who half strangled me, and you brought me here as your prisoner," I said.

"Tell us, does Drake also believe that the moon is made of cheese?" Harry said in that low, smooth voice.

Zoe giggled from within the darkness.

I knew he was mocking me for even believing Drake's theories. Then Harry's voice turned harsh as I saw his large frame move across the room towards me. "How do we know you're not the killer?"

"What?" I gasped. "That's nonsense."

"Is it?" Harry said, his voice now sounding like a growl. "It is you who have recently come from London where you claim to have chased this killer onto a train. It is you who the preacher found alone in the desert, claiming that you had lost your memory. You were left alone in the town of Black Water Gap while we were shackled and being watched by Louise. You arrived in Silent Rest just like the rest of us, and none of us saw you until dusk."

"I was asleep in my room, hungover from the night . . . " I started.

"So *you* say," Harry barked, and just for a moment, in the weak glowing light from the lamp, I saw a flash of his bright yellow eyes and I took a step backwards.

"Zoe found me in my room," I protested. "I'd just woken up."

"Is this true, Zoe?" Harry growled.

"Yes," she said from the darkness.

"And I've never been to the town Crows Ranch," I said, feeling now is if I did have something to hide. "The preacher found me."

"But where had you been and where had you come from before the preacher discovered you?" Harry came back at me.

"I'd come from London!" I shouted back at him, my fists clenched.

"And so had this killer," Harry said. "These killings didn't start until you arrived here."

"I know what you're thinking . . . " I started, feeling as if I were on trial. But what was my defence and who would believe me?

"Why are you here, Sammy?" the preacher suddenly spoke up. "Has your memory returned yet?"

"No," I whispered, knowing that I was fast running out of excuses. "All I know is what I've already told you. I was chasing a man who I believed to be a killer, he put his arm about my throat, told me that I had forgotten, and the next thing I know, I'm shooting down five men in the desert."

"What had you forgotten?" Harry asked me.

"Sorry?"

"This man, the one who put his arm about your throat, he said that you had forgotten," Harry said. "What did he mean?"

"I don't know," I said shaking my head.

"It seems that you don't know very much," Louise said from beside me. "Perhaps you are this killer."

"I'm not a killer!" I screeched at them all. "Just leave me alone." I felt tears begin to swell in the corners of my eyes and splash onto my cheeks. Then, drawing a deep breath, and with my lower lip trembling, I said, "You're right, there is a lot of stuff that I don't know. Like I don't know how I can fire a gun, I'd never even seen one until I arrived in this godforsaken place. I'd never ridden a horse; there was a donkey once, but that doesn't count. I don't know how I managed to kill five men in a blink of an eye. But what I really don't know is how a girl from the year two-thousand-and-twelve has ended up lost and bewildered in eighteen-eighty-eight!"

There was a silence, which seemed to drag out for ever. Then slowly, I saw the preacher's shadow flicker across the lamplight as he rose from his chair. He came towards me.

"I asked you this question once before, Sammy,

and I'll ask you only once more," he whispered, his breath cold against my face, "What year were you born?"

"I was born in nineteen-ninety," I whispered, and just to say that was like having a huge weight lifted from me. I just couldn't lie anymore. I just couldn't keep up the pretence. And if these people – these *Skinturners* as they called themselves – were just a figment of my imagination – then did it really matter if they believed me or not? I wasn't sure if I really cared anymore. Perhaps if the truth was out, I could go home.

"Perhaps you hit your head harder than I first thought," the preacher breathed into my face.

"I'm telling you the truth," I said back, wiping the tears from my face with the backs of my hands.

"What, that you really live one hundred and twenty four years from now? You want me to believe that?" he whispered, like it was a private conversation just between us.

"Yes," I sniffed. "I'm telling you the truth."

"She doesn't have nuthin' under her hat but hair," Harry mocked.

Ignoring his remark, I looked at the black shape of the preacher before me and said, "I thought you were a man of faith, Preacher?"

"How can I have faith in a story such as yours?" he hissed, and I could smell stale tobacco on his breath.

"Did Jesus walk on water?" I snapped back.

"Stop . . . " the preacher growled, but I continued.

"Did he heal the sick, feed the starving, did he cheat death and rise on the third day . . . "

"Stop this blasphemy!" the preacher howled as if I had struck him.

"You believe he did all of those things, but were you there? Did you witness those miracles with your own eyes?" I challenged him.

"Of course not!"

"But you still believe he did all of those things because you have *faith*," I told him. "I don't have any wounds to show you like Jesus did for Thomas. I can't prove that I'm telling you the truth. All I'm asking is you have some *faith* in me."

"But it's unbelievable," Louise said.

"Any more believable than me standing in a train, halfway up a mountain, talking to a bunch of freaking werewolves?" I spat.

"If what you say is true, then why are you here?" I heard Zoe ask me.

"I don't know why," I said. "I'm beginning to think it has something to do with the killings which have been taking place. The killings back where I'm from and the killings here. I'm starting to believe that they are connected somehow."

Then out of the darkness, I saw the preacher's eyes shining just inches from my face like two crescent moons. "Maybe you were right, *future-girl,* about this man who you say you chased onto that train one hundred and twenty four years from now."

"What do you mean?" I whispered, unable to stop myself from staring into his eyes.

"Perhaps the killer is a vampire and he is responsible for the killings here and in your world," he said. "Maybe you have been sent back to stop him, and to stop the killings from happening one hundred and twenty four years from now."

"You believe me, don't you?" I whispered.

"I believe that you *believe*," he said, and although I couldn't see his face, I knew in my heart that he was smiling.

Looking back into those crescent moon-shaped eyes, which glistened in the darkness before me, I said, "But why me?"

"Why not?" he whispered, and the brightness in his eyes winked out, leaving only darkness.

"I couldn't give a rat's-ass whether you're telling the truth or not," Harry growled from out of the dark. "But what does matter is that Drake believes the preacher is responsible for killing those women and we helped him."

"I know that you didn't kill those women," I said to the preacher as his silhouette shifted across the carriage. "I know none of you were involved."

"Thanks for your support, but I think it's a bit too late in the day for that," Louise said.

"I can help you," I told them. "We can help each

other. We both need to catch this killer, right? You, to prove your innocence, and me, to stop future killings from taking place."

"So what's your plan?" Zoe asked me. Her voice came from the other side of the carriage as if she had moved in the darkness without me realising.

"I don't have a plan," I told her. "But Drake does."

"Tell us," Harry barked, his voice booming. Again I noticed how different he sounded as a wolfman. Did he look just like the preacher had? Had he lost those annoyingly rugged good looks? I wondered.

"He has set a trap," I told them.

"What kind?" the preacher asked.

"When we get to The Hanging Mine, there are going to be police officers and the Marshal from Silent Rest waiting to take you into custody," I confessed.

"Or kill us," Harry barked at the preacher.

"We should get off this train – right now," Zoe said.

"No," the preacher whispered. "We stay on the train. We can't get off. We haven't fully changed, so we will die in the light."

"We're trapped then," Louise spoke up.

"Not necessarily," the preacher said thoughtfully. "I have a plan of my own."

32

The preacher sent me to see Drake with a message. I told Drake that I had seen the preacher and the others re-board the train, and that they had gone straight to their berths. Drake wasn't surprised by this, and rubbing his hands together with glee, he smiled at me.

"What did I tell you, Miss Carter? Vampires – all of them are! We won't see them again until this evening, by which time we would have reached The Hanging Mines." Then turning to the doctor who stood beside him, he said, "Let's get this train moving again!"

I left Drake to return to his own berth and I went back to my own. I pushed open the door to find my carriage still shrouded in darkness.

"I've passed on your message," I whispered.

There was no reply. I didn't need one; I knew that they had gone. *But where?* I wondered. I didn't know what the preacher had planned – he hadn't told me. Why not? Did it have something to do with the *faith* thing again? I guessed so.

Pulling back the curtains just an inch, I let a slice of sunlight into my room. I felt tired, but my mind raced with the night's events and I knew it would be some time before I slept – if at all. On the table next to the armchair where the preacher had hidden in the dark, I found two of his hand-rolled cigarettes and a book of matches. I popped one of the cigarettes in the corner of my mouth and opened the matches. There were just two. Short and white with little black bulbous heads. It was then I saw a short message scribbled on the inside flap of the matchbook.

Two smokes – two matches!
Save one of them!

Not knowing what the message meant, and too damned tired to even try and figure it out, I tore off one of the matches and lit the cigarette I had stuck in the corner of my mouth. *One of each left*, I thought as I blew out the match.

I settled back into the armchair, and picking up the copy of *A Study in Scarlet* by Sir Arthur Conan Doyle, I started to read. I hoped that it might take my mind off everything I had seen and learnt since arriving in 1888.

I woke with a start. It felt like the whole world had been violently shaken. With eyes wide, I looked about the carriage and realised that the train had come to a stop. I was alone and slumped in the armchair where I must have fallen asleep. The book I'd been reading was in my lap. On the table sat the match and the cigarette. I placed the book of matches in my shirt pocket and tucked the cigarette behind my ear.

I went to the window and peered out. It was dusk, and the sun was slipping slowly behind the tops of the mountains in the distance, like a blood-red eye. Just like I had seen before, the sun's crimson rays poured through the giant gorges and crevices in the mountains, giving the appearance of hundreds of blood-filled rivers flowing over and between them. I peered left and right along the length of the train and could see that Drake's crew was disembarking from the train. There were shouts and orders being passed along the line of workers as they lifted the trunks from the train that they had carried on at the start of our journey. I watched as they led our horses from the carriage with the giant wooden dropdown door. The horses neighed and stomped their hooves into the ground, kicking up plumes of dust. I saw them bring out Moon, and he pulled at the handler who was trying to lead him from the train.

I put on my hat, filled the empty clips on my belt with the bullets Harry had stolen from the gunsmith's, and loaded the chambers of my two revolvers. With my long dark brown coat flapping about my calves, and not knowing what the night would bring, I left my carriage and climbed from the train.

33

Moon was neighing and still pulling at the reins as I approached the guy in the bowler hat who was trying to tame the horse.

"You don't handle him like that," I said.

He looked at me and said nothing. He had a finely trimmed moustache, which was black. He was smartly dressed in a grey tweed suit and I guessed that he was one of the police officers Drake was hoping to use to snare the preacher and the others. I tried to take the reins from him, but he glared at me and snatched his hand away.

"Hey, back off!" I scowled at him. "This is my horse."

The guy stood and stared back at me.

"Let her take it," Drake said, and I turned around to find him standing behind me, leaning against his walking stick. The dying sun was so bright, at first I thought he had a long black shadow trailing out behind him. But holding a hand up to my eyes, it was the doctor who I could see standing just behind him.

The officer handed me the reins, and stroking Moon's muzzle, I calmed him.

"If I were you, Miss Carter, I would saddle up and ride as far away from here as possible," Drake said. "Go back to London."

"I don't think I can go back," I told him. "Besides, I want to stay and see if what you say is right about the preacher and his friends. I need to know if the preacher really is who you claim him to be."

"Why?" Drake said, sounding curious.

"I've put a lot of faith in the preacher, and I want to see if it has been misplaced like you claim it to be," I told him.

"Have it your way," he smiled at me.

The train had now been unloaded, and the trunks, suitcases, and empty crates stood neatly piled by the engine of the *Scorpion Steam*, which trailed a thick line of black smoke up into the red sky. The mountains that seemed to tower above us on all sides gave me the feeling that our journey had ended in a deep valley. Moon kicked at the hard stony ground, and spying a solitary tree to my left, I could see the other horses had been tethered to it. I led my horse towards the others and it was then that I saw the gaping mouth of a tunnel which led deep into the mountainside. Above the ragged-looking opening, someone had fixed a wooden sign which read *The Hanging Mine*. Next to the opening, I saw several boxes of what looked like sticks of dynamite, and I guessed these had been used to blow open the mine.

As I tethered Moon to the dried-out-looking tree trunk, I saw movement in the entrance to the mine. At first I couldn't figure out what it was, but then from the darkness stepped a broad-shouldered man, and another who was dressed similar to the preacher. The first wore a Stetson, had a shiny silver star-shaped badge fixed to his shirt just above his heart, and had a gun belt criss-crossed about his waist. In his hands he carried a rifle. The priest was older-looking than the Marshal and his bald head reflected back the dying rays of the blood-red sun. In his hands he clutched a Bible, and a set of rosary beads were entwined about his fingers. Both walked over to Drake and the doctor and I joined them, interested to find out what was being said.

The guys in the bowler hats with the neatly trimmed moustaches stood in a neat line by the train. "These are some of my finest officers," Drake said to the Marshal, gesturing towards his men.

The Marshal eyed them and then grunted, "I've received word from Silent Rest that this man – creature – has taken my wife's life. Is this true?"

"I'm afraid so, Marshal," Drake said, a forlorn look on his face.

Hearing this, the priest made the sign of the cross and gently touched the Marshal's arm.

"Take courage," the priest said, as if trying to comfort the man.

Shrugging the priest free of him, the Marshal roared, "I'll take his head! Where is this beast?"

"Asleep on board the train, as are the others," Drake said.

"Well let's not waste any more time," the Marshal barked. "Let's get them off."

Drake turned to the doctor and said, "You know what to do."

Then as if planned, the officers lined up beside the train, drew their guns, and followed the doctor on board.

Drake shot me a look, and I stared back at him. With the priest mumbling to himself as he read from the Bible, which now lay open in his hands, I watched the doctor climb from the train and come rushing over to Drake.

"They're not on board!"

What do you mean they're not on board?" Drake snapped. "They couldn't have gotten off; the sun is yet to fully fade."

"They're not on the train," the doctor insisted, a look of concern on his face.

"Check and then check again!" Drake shouted at the officers who were disembarking the train. They abruptly turned and climbed back on.

"They're wasting their time," the doctor hissed at Drake. "They've gone, I'm telling you."

"Impossible," Drake snapped.

"Maybe they fled as soon as we stopped," the doctor suggested and I couldn't help but notice the panic in his eyes.

"Their horses are still here, so they couldn't have gone far. The light is fading fast," he said to the doctor. "Take the men with you and go find them before it turns dark."

Without saying another word, the doctor raced back towards the train and now demanded that the officers get off once again. I watched them clamber down the iron steps and into the dust. They looked confused and lost. Wherever the preacher and the others had gone – whatever their plan – they were already throwing Drake and his men into utter confusion.

"Do you think this is funny?" Drake suddenly spat at me.

I didn't realise I'd been smiling as I watched the doctor and the others scurry away in search of my friends. "No," I said trying to mask my smirk.

"You told him, didn't you?" Drake breathed, coming towards me, his walking stick in hand. "You warned all of them."

"Did not," I lied.

"Is she one of 'em?" the Marshal asked, pointing his gun at me.

"I thought not," Drake whispered, looking into my eyes, "but now I'm not so sure."

I looked back into his perfect green eyes.

"You told them, didn't you?" he asked again.

"The preacher didn't kill any of those women," I said. "He isn't Jack the Ripper."

"And what do you know?" He sneered, the corners of his mouth twitching.

"I've been doing some thinking," I said. "How did the preacher or any of the others travel from London to here so quickly?"

"What are you talking about?" he asked, his eyes narrowing.

"Where I come from, it would take six days for a ship to travel from Southampton in England to New York," I said. "But from there to here, I'm guessing about a month or more."

"What's going on?" the Marshal asked, striding towards us, his rifle raised.

Without taking my eyes from Drake, I said, "Mary Jane Kelly, the last of the Ripper's victims to be murdered in London, died on November the 9th, that was the day I woke in up in the desert. That was the day I first met the preacher."

"You don't know what you're talking about," Drake sneered.

"I remember asking the preacher what the day was as I travelled with him and the others to the town of Black Water Gap – it was the 12th of November – still only three days after the Ripper's last killing in London."

"You're confused," Drake said. I could tell that he was pissed off because I was picking his theory about the preacher to pieces and he knew it. "He lied about the date."

"He didn't," I said calmly. "The date on the newspaper in which I read about the murder that had taken place in Crows Ranch was dated the 12th of November. Therefore, the preacher couldn't have possibly committed the murders in London – he couldn't have travelled across the Atlantic Ocean so quickly."

"Are you stupid?" Drake snapped at me. "Didn't you listen to a word that I told you? The preacher and the others are vampires. They can change into mist, vapour, and fog. They could have made that journey in a blink of an eye if they had wanted to. Travelled like the wind if they had needed to."

"But the preacher and his friends aren't vampires," I told him. "Now that is one thing I do know for sure." Then, as I watched Drake eye me with contempt, my fingers twitched over my guns as I said, "So how did you get to be here so quickly after the death of Mary Jane Kelly?"

"What are you talking about, child?" Drake shot back at me.

"That day I first saw you in the saloon," I reminded him. "You said that just before leaving London, you read in the newspaper about the Ripper's last killing." Then realising what I was suggesting, I gasped and added, "So how did you and the doctor get here so quickly?"

There was a deathly silence as Drake stared at me, a sudden and beautiful smile forming on his lips.

With his brow furrowed with deep lines, the Marshal cut in and said, "What is going on here?" Then glancing at Drake, he added, "I thought you said this preacher was responsible for the murder of five women back in England and here? You've just told me he was the creature who killed my wife."

"He didn't kill your wife. I did," a voice suddenly spoke up, and we all turned around.

34

The doctor stood by the train as the sun cast its last rays of light across the darkening sky and snow-flecked mountaintops. Slowly, he came towards us. The Marshal stood beside me, his face now a mask of total confusion. The priest kissed his rosary beads and crossed himself. Without even knowing how they had got there, my guns were in my fists and trained on the doctor. Drake stared at his companion, looking as shocked as the rest of us.

"What are you saying?" Drake asked him. "Have you been struck by madness?"

"I think it's time we stopped with the pretence, don't you, brother?" the doctor smiled at Drake.

"Brother?" I whispered.

"I'm afraid so," Drake said from beside me.

"I couldn't give a damn who's related to who," the Marshal barked. "Did you kill my wife?"

"Her liver was a bit spongy," the doctor smiled at the Marshal. "She must have drunk far too much liquor in her life. But then again, there have been a lot of women who have described me as a fancy *licker*," and he laughed like a child telling a rude joke.

"Why, you filthy dog!" the Marshal roared, raising his rifle and taking aim. There was an ear-splitting *BANG* which echoed back off the mountains. I looked up, expecting to see the doctor's brains splashed across the side of the train. But he had gone, vanished – or so I thought. The Marshal started to scream and I swung around to find the doctor astride the Marshal's back. It looked surreal, as if the Marshal was giving him a piggyback ride. The Marshal had dropped his rifle and was frantically clawing at the air, desperate to remove the doctor, who now had his face buried in the Marshal's neck.

Blood jetted from the Marshal's open mouth in a thick, black stream. His screams turned to a series of rasping cries as he fought with the doctor. I raised my guns and took aim, but Drake was as quick as his brother and snatched them from me in a blink of an eye. The priest screamed and staggered backwards as a clot of blood shot from the Marshal's open throat and spattered his face.

"Dear, sweet Jesus," the priest cried, holding up his

rosary beads. Then his head was gone from his shoulders in an explosion of shattered skull fragments, flesh, and brain. I looked at Drake, who stood holding my guns, wispy lines of smoke trailing up from each of them.

"He's with the Lord now," he smiled at me. "I'm sure his rewards will be great."

"What sort of person are you?" I cried, stumbling backwards.

The Marshal dropped to the ground in a puff of dust. The doctor stood up and wiped a stringy red lump of flesh from his chin with the sleeve of his dark suit.

"Marcus," Drake breathed. "Was it really you who killed all of those women?"

"Yes, Spencer," Marcus said, picking a piece of flesh from between his teeth with a fingernail.

"You bloody fool!" Drake snapped. "You could've ruined everything!"

"Ruined what?" I dared to ask.

Wheeling around, Drake looked at me and said, "It wasn't meant to be like this. Not the murders of all those women. It could have brought attention to us and our plan."

"So let me get this straight," I gasped. "You're not pissed at your psycho brother because he butchered all those women . . . "

"No, not really," Drake shrugged.

"You're just mad at him because he might have ruined some plan, whatever that might be," I continued.

258

"Yes. Why, have you got a problem with that?" he snapped at me.

"So you're not like a real copper after all?" I said, trying to play catch-up.

"I am a police officer, and I was hunting a killer," he said.

"I think your hunt is over. The killer's standing right over there," I said, pointing at the doctor. And to look at him, it made sense. The police had always suspected that the killer had been a medical practitioner of some kind, as he had removed the victim's internal organs with such precision. The apron, a surgeon's gown.

"Why, Marcus?" he said, turning on his brother. "Why have you done this?"

I was confused because Drake actually sounded as startled and as lost as I did.

"Didn't you suspect me at all?" Marcus asked, licking the last of the Marshal's blood from his fingers.

"No," Drake said with a weary shake of his head. "I thought you wanted an end to the killing, like me. I thought we were hunting the one who will turn the vampires against us. I thought our plan was to help him become civilised. Show him he can live amongst the humans, as we do."

"But they were just human women," Marcus laughed, as if not understanding what all the fuss was about.

Hearing this, Drake suddenly struck his brother up the side of his head with the butt of one of my guns.

There was sickening thud and Marcus threw his hands to his face.

"I'm so sorry, brother," he wailed, dropping to his knees like a child. He then gripped the hems of Drake's trousers and snivelled. "I tried to stop what I was doing, I really did. You have to believe me. But I can't help myself. It's like a sickness. Help me, brother. Don't punish me."

"You're the reason why vampires have to hide away, only come out in the night," Drake raged down at him. "You disgust me."

"Please," Marcus sobbed, looking up into his brother's eyes. "I love you. I would be nothing without you."

Drake said nothing. He stood silently. Then, when his brother's pitiful sobs became unbearable, he snatched his brother up and held him. Marcus cried against his brother's chest.

"Shhh," Drake soothed him, his anger now ebbing away. "I will cure you of this sickness. I promise you, little brother."

"You said that you were chasing someone else for the murders," I said, feeling sick at the brothers' twisted and misguided love for one another. "So you don't believe the preacher is the killer?"

"No, I never have," Drake smiled, turning on me.

"So why trap him, bring him out to this mine, if you never believed him to be a killer, if you were hunting someone else?" I asked.

"There are vampires who don't want our help," Drake said. "They are ruled by the one who calls himself the Soulless Liege. He enjoys the slaying of humans and the drinking of their blood. We want more than that. I want to lead a civilised life, a life where I don't have to hide by day, and hunt at night. I'm tired of waiting for a human to drive a stake through my heart as I sleep. So I was speaking the truth when I said I wanted the preacher's protection. Sadly, he and his team are the best vampire hunters there are. All of them are legends in the supernatural world that both our species inhabit – but there can only be one."

"So those vampires who attacked us in Silent Rest . . ." I started.

"Were sent by the Soulless Liege to stop us," Drake cut in, as his brother cowered pathetically behind him.

"So once the preacher had gotten you this far, what was the plan?" I snipped at him.

"To hand them over to the Marshal to be hung for the murders of those women," he said.

"So the real killer, this *Pale Liege* who you suspected, could get away," I asked, his plan finally falling into place for me.

"He wouldn't have gotten away," Drake said. "We had come to help him change his ways. To see that there was another way for all of us."

"So you were going to help him, like you promised to help your brother," I sneered in disgust at the pair of them. "You would have let the preacher and the others hang for a crime committed by one of your own. Why?"

"Because the preacher and his outlaw friends are nothing but filthy Skinturners," he smiled. "And they hunt me and my kind down. They are the last of their breed and they stand in the way of what we want. But they are gone now, scattered to the wind like the cowards they are."

Then, coming towards me, one of my guns in his fist, he looked at me and said, "Poor Samantha Carter, deserted by the preacher – the man who she put all of her faith in. Perhaps you could join us instead," he smiled showing two pointed teeth at each corner of his mouth. He threw my guns away, knowing that he wouldn't need them. "I can give you eternal life, Sammy. You really are so beautiful – you belong with us – not with wolves."

"No," I spat. "Vampires don't offer eternal life. The preacher told me that."

"But where is the preacher now?" he smiled, closing the gap between us.

"I'm right here, Drake," I heard the preacher suddenly say.

Drake and I both turned around, and with my heart thumping in my chest, I could have screamed with joy, as the lids to the large wooden trunks, which had been taken from the train, flew open. The preacher and my friends leapt from them, guns in hand.

35

Drake tried to hide his surprise by clapping his hands together and smiling.

"Bravo! Bravo!" Drake said. "You have done well." He stooped down and picked up his cane, which he had dropped when seizing my guns.

"Those who seek shall find," the preacher said, his guns aimed straight at Drake's head. I glanced at the others. Harry had that mean look on his face as he trained his guns on the doctor. Louise looked at me and gave me a sly wink and Zoe had that same angry frown I had seen on her face in Silent Rest.

Oh, my God – I knew what was coming and it was going to be bad. My eyes scanned the ground and I saw my pistols lying in the dust about ten feet away. It was dark now and the sky was full of slow moving clouds. But even so, I could see my friends' clothes all appeared to be covered in a fine grey dust.

"You may as well lay down you guns, Preacher Man," Drake smiled with a newfound confidence, as if he knew something the rest of us didn't.

"How do you figure that?" the preacher asked, and although I couldn't see his mouth under the big droopy moustache, I knew that he wasn't smiling. I inched sideways towards my guns. Marcus was watching his brother.

"We are standing at the mouth of The Hanging Mines," Drake said, "Just one of thousands of Vrykolaka's nests." Looking up at the night sky, he added, "In just a few moments they will rise, and you will be vastly outnumbered. Let my brother and me end it for you now. We promise to make it quick – as painless as possible."

"From what I heard you say from the trunk, and how they came after us at Silent Rest," the preacher said, his eyes an icy blue, "The Vrykolakas aren't going to welcome you, either."

"Oh, but they will," Drake smiled. "I come with an offer of a new existence for them – a new life. A life where they don't have to live in caves during the day like vermin, creeping out at night just to feed. I can give them so much more than that."

"It doesn't sound like your King is interested," the preacher said, his guns not wavering an inch.

"Have you not wondered how I've been able to reflect

in mirrors?" Then glancing at me he added, "How I passed your little test with the holy water? How I have managed to create a life for me and my brother, living amongst the humans in London?"

I shook my head and slowly inched towards my guns.

"Science," Drake smiled back at the others, who still stood before the empty trunks. They hadn't moved an inch since making their sudden appearance – they looked like statues. "You think my brother is a savage – a killer. And yes, I do admit that he can get carried away a little at times. But he has one of the greatest scientific minds of our age. Thanks to my brother's tireless energies and research . . . "

"And ripping the guts out of innocent women. Is that what you would call medical research?" Harry cut in.

Drake ignored him and continued, " . . . through tireless research, my brother has created a salve which, when rubbed into the flesh, will give us the ability to reflect, be immune to blessed water and other trinkets that humans might use to repel us."

"What is he talking about?" Zoe asked Louise from the corner of her mouth.

Without taking her eyes off her target, Marcus, Louise shrugged.

"What I think Drake is trying to tell us," I said, "is that he and his little brother have created some kind of vampire sunblock. Where I come from, L'Oreal would snap him and his brother up in a blink of an eye."

"Sunblock?" Zoe asked Louise again from the corner of her mouth.

Again Louise shrugged.

"What a great name!" Drake smiled at me, and clapped his hands. "Sunblock! You really should be one of us, Sammy."

"No thanks," I smiled back, and inched further towards my guns in the dirt.

Drake's face took on a sad kind of look as he said, "I like the name, but the salve's ability to block out the sun has limited effects. As you have seen, I have been unable to masquerade in the light. When I met you at the saloon, I had to keep to the shadows, and also when I disembarked from the train at dusk today. The effects wear off rather too quickly and we blister and peel, our skin weeps, and . . . "

"Look, we know how all of that feels," the preacher said impatiently. "You're preaching to the converted."

"So what's the missing ingredient?" I quizzed him.

Looking at me, Drake smiled and said, "Gold. And these mines are rich with it."

Stepping out from his brother's shadow, Marcus said, "England is rich in many of the minerals I've needed, but there really is no gold. I've experimented by melting down rings, necklaces, and bracelets. But like my brother has explained – it is not enough. We need so much more, and the mines in these mountains will provide us with that."

"So you see," Drake smiled, "when the Vrykolakas rise in just mere moments and I show them the salve and how it will let them live as human equals and not vermin, they will welcome us, whatever the Soulless Liege says. I will be their new king. I will be more than that, I will be their saviour."

"I can only think of one true saviour," the preacher said, "and look what the people he came to save did to him."

"Enough of the Sunday School teachings," Drake sneered. "You're no holy man. You're just like us. Creatures of the night, of the shadows, cast out and hunted down like animals by humans. But tonight that stops and a new era is born. Unlike your saviour, I do not turn the other cheek, I don't pity the weak, I show no mercy, and I never ever show forgiveness." Then in a blinding flash, he pulled a long, razor-thin, silver sword hidden within his walking stick and sliced his brother's head from his shoulders.

With my hands clasped to my mouth in shock, I watched Marcus's head fly through the air, his eyes wide open, and mouth opening and closing as if trying to say something. The head bounced into the dirt, rolling over and over, its long black hair gathering dust, making it look white. Marcus's head came to rest on one cheek, and his dead eyes stared at me, a permanent look of shock for ever on his face.

The preacher and the others looked unmoved by

what they had just seen, all of their guns now trained on Drake.

"You just killed your own brother," I gasped, not out of pity for Marcus, but because I knew – *I hoped* – that if I had come back to 1888 to prevent the killings taking place in 2012, Drake had just unwittingly stopped them for me. But if that was so – if my mission was accomplished – shouldn't I be waking up at any moment, back on that tube train?

Why am I still here? I wondered. "Why?" I shouted out aloud.

"Why?" Drake said, "Marcus was drawing unwanted attention to me. He has the entire Metropolitan Police Force hunting a killer – him – and it would have only been a matter of time before they snared him, and that would have led them to me. I'm not going to be caught because my little brother couldn't resist the urge to murder filthy whores."

"They were women," I breathed, hoping that I was going to wake up in 2012 at any moment.

"Like I've already said, I don't do forgiveness," he smiled with a shrug. "That was my father's mistake. He should have murdered my brother at birth."

"Why?" I asked him.

"He killed my mother, clawing his way out of her womb," Drake sighed. "All very nasty."

"But if it hadn't of been for your brother, you wouldn't have this . . . " Zoe started, then looking

268

at me, she added, "what did you say it was called?"

"Sunblock," I said back, still hoping that I was going to be snatched back to 2012 at any moment.

"Yeah, that," Zoe said.

"I agree, Marcus had his uses," Drake mused, walking towards his brother's head and prodding at it with the toe of his boot. "He would have done anything for me. But I know the formula now and what I need to add."

"So where is this stuff?" Harry grunted.

"You've just been lying in it," Drake grinned back at him. "I wonder if it has the same effect on blocking out moonlight." Drake clapped his hands together again and laughed.

"You mean that grey flaky powder which was in these four trunks is the *magic* powder you were bringing up here to the mountains?" Harry asked.

"That's right," Drake nodded.

"Oh, shit," Harry said, trying to hide a smile. "I'm really sorry, because if I'd have known how important the stuff was to you, I would've never emptied it all out of the train door about forty miles back."

"What are you talking about?" Drake said, the smile fading from his lips.

"Don't panic just yet, Drake," Harry said looking over at the preacher. "Did you empty your trunk, too?"

"Sure did," the preacher said, not taking his eyes from Drake. "The stuff stank."

Then turning to look at Louise and Zoe, Harry said,

"What about you two? You didn't throw it all away, did you?"

"Yep," they said as one.

"Oh, boy, I'm really sorry about this. It's really kind of embarrassing because it looks like we chucked all that stuff out," Harry said with a mocking look of concern on his face. "Was it, like, really expensive to make, because you know, I'm sure we could all have a collection or summin' so you could go and buy some more, I think I've got a few dollars tucked away somewhere."

"Looks like you killed your brother too soon," the preacher said, his guns never moving from Drake.

"You knew what that stuff was," Drake seethed, his eyes narrowing into angry slits.

"Maybe we did, and maybe we didn't," the preacher shrugged. "It's all gone now. So what'cha gonna do, Drake?"

Before Drake had a chance to reply, the officers, who had earlier gone in search of my friends, came running back along the track towards us, guns at the ready.

"*Fire!*" Drake roared at them.

The whole mountainside began to shake and rumble. But it wasn't the sound of gunfire I could hear. It was something moving at speed, deep within the mine behind us.

36

Everything seemed to happen at once. Drake turned to look back at the mouth of the mine. As the sound of gunfire boomed all around me, I seized my chance by leaping the last few feet to my guns and snatching them up off the ground. Spinning around, I began to fire at the approaching officers as they headed up the tracks. Harry was racing towards them, his arms out front, revolvers smoking in his fists. Bullets whizzed and zinged all around me, columns of dust flying up in the air as wayward bullets thudded into the ground at my feet.

Louise dived behind one of the trunks, and with her head low, she raised her arms above the lid and emptied her guns on the approaching lawmen. Two of them flew back into the air, their feet lifting clean off the ground as Louise's bullets thudded into them. I looked back to see Zoe race at an amazing speed towards her horse, which was still tethered to the tree. Running at it from behind, I watched Zoe leap into the air and mount the horse. With one clean swipe of what looked like a claw, she cut the tether in two, turned her horse, and galloped towards the officers who were now at the rear of the train. Bent forward in her saddle, her head resting against the horse's neck, Zoe fired her guns at the officers who shot back at her from behind the train. Harry raced towards them, faster and faster. Nearing the last carriage where the officers crouched, he leapt into the air and scrambled onto the roof. As I watched him, I could see that his hands now looked more like claws. As he bounded across the roof of the observation carriage, he fired into the glass, dropping out of sight. Within moments I heard the sound of screaming and saw sheets of blood, limbs, and entrails flying into the sky from behind the carriage. The officers' screams were then drowned out by the sound of howling.

Some of the officers cut free and ran blindly out from behind the train. From her horse, Zoe picked them off as her guns thundered in her fists. Two others ran in frantic circles, firing their guns at everything and nothing. Popping up from behind the trunk, Louise fired, and the last remaining men flew backwards, their faces spraying the side of the train in a mosaic of red.

Where was the preacher? I wondered. I hadn't seen him since the gunfight had started. I turned to see him stacking the sticks of dynamite, which I had earlier noticed, against the wall outside the mouth of the mine.

Looking back at me, the preacher roared, "Do you have the match I left for you?"

"Right here!" I yelled, taking it from my shirt pocket. I knelt down by the preacher and helped him stack the sticks in bundles at the opening of the mine. "I have one cigarette left if you want to share it," I half-smiled at the preacher.

"Later," he smiled back from beneath his moustache.

We were then joined by the others as each of them started to frantically stack the sticks of dynamite. I glanced at Harry's hands as he worked, and I could see that they looked like hands again, but he had blood on them.

From deep within the mine, I heard the sound of screeching. It sounded terrifying, like a thousand demons were clawing their way out of the earth. "Where did Drake disappear to?" I asked as I worked.

"He went into the mine," the preacher said. "So if we go and blow the goddamn thing up, we take him and the vampires together and . . ."

But before he had finished, a deep growling sound came from the back of his throat. At first I wondered if it was the echo of the vampires deep within the mine that I could hear. The sound came again, and this time it was from behind me. I wheeled around to see Harry and Zoe collapse to the ground. Just like they had the night before on the roof of the train, they looked as if they were throwing a fit.

"We've got to chain them up," Louise snapped, her eyes wide, brimming with fear.

As I looked up at her, I could see the clouds parting and the full moon shining out from behind. Harry rolled onto his side, clutching his stomach, and his eyes rolled back in their sockets. I looked down at him, and part of me wanted to go to him.

As if reading my thoughts, Louise shouted at me. "You can't help him! You can't help any of them!"

With my heart racing in my chest, I watched, open mouthed, as Harry rolled onto his back. He thrust his hands out as if reaching for me, a thick howling noise coming from the back of his throat. It echoed back off the mountains, and was so loud that my bones almost seemed to rattle beneath my flesh. Harry's hands began to twist out of shape, and I could hear the sounds of his knuckles breaking as his fingers turned into long, hooked claws. Thick lengths of coarse brown hair oozed from the backs of his hands and face. His nose turned upwards and his jaw stretched as the lower half of his face took on the form of a giant wolf. His eyeballs rolled down, and they glowed yellow.

"Don't just stand there!" Louise roared, tearing me from my trance.

I looked at her, dropping the stick of dynamite that I had in my hand. Then, from the corner of my eye,

I saw a blazing flash of fur cross my field of vision. I looked at Louise as Zoe knocked her to the ground. Zoe's long blond hair was now darker and thicker somehow, and billowed about in the wind. Her face stretched and contorted as she sunk her teeth into Louise's shoulder. Louise reached for her guns, but Zoe had clattered into her with such force, her guns spun from her hands.

With a blur of movement, I had drawn my own guns and was aiming both of them at Zoe, who was now burying her muzzle into Louise's shoulder. Blood spattered her face, and seeing my guns aimed at Zoe, Louise screamed, "No! Don't kill her!"

With the sound of the screeching vampires echoing from within the mine, and the ear-splitting howling coming from Harry, I spun around to see the preacher roll onto all fours like a giant dog. He arched his shoulders as if having a violent spasm and threw his head back. His whole face shot forward as it took on the shape of a wolf. He opened his mouth and howled as a set of pointed teeth tore out of his gums.

I stumbled backwards towards the mine, and was grabbed from behind. Screaming, I kicked wildly backwards, as my guns were yanked from my hands and thrown out of reach.

"I can save you," Drake breathed into my ear, pulling back into the darkness of the mine.

"I don't want to be saved by you or your kind!" I

shrieked as I fought with him. But he was too strong and easily overpowered me. He threw me against the wall of the mine, striking my head.

He looked back into the tunnel as the sound of the approaching vampires grew ever louder. "Become one of us," Drake smiled, his face so close to mine that our lips were almost touching.

"Never!" I screamed, my heart beating like a trip hammer in my chest.

"If you don't become like me, you become one of them," he said, looking out at where my friends were howling and snarling.

I glanced sideways and could see that they had almost completed their change. The preacher was standing at least seven foot tall on a set of white hair-covered hind legs. Two long arms swung at his sides, and his face was like that of giant wolf. Long white whiskers hung from his glistening snout. Throwing back his head, he beat his chest with his claws and howled so loud that I thought my eardrums might just burst.

"Is that what you want to become?" Drake hissed into my face.

"If it means not turning out like you, then yes," I sneered back into Drake's face.

Throwing me to the ground, he sat astride me as the first wave of vampires leapt over us and out into the night. I heard the preacher howl again, but it was too difficult to truly know what was happening as I saw shiny claws slashing back and forth in the moonlight outside. I looked right down into the mine as the vampires raced forward, and just like the vampires I had seen in Silent Rest, their mouths were huge gaping wounds in their faces, their eyes red and burning.

I looked up into Drake's face and screamed. Just like the others, his face had now changed to look just like theirs. His festering mouth ran from ear to ear, his black swollen gums crammed with razor-sharp teeth.

How had I ever thought his mouth had looked so kissable, I wondered as he lent over me. His skin had turned a chalky white, and I could see a maze of blue and green veins pulsating beneath his skin.

"If you won't give yourself to me, then I will take you," Drake said, his voice now rasping and screechy.

Pinning me to the ground with his knees, he pulled open the front of his suit and I gasped at the sight of the blood-covered apron which hid there. I looked at his now long, pointed fingers, and his claws looked like knives.

"You're the Ripper," I gasped. "It wasn't your brother."

"I know," he grinned, that huge mouth of his twisting into a deformed smile.

"But why did Marcus confess when it was you?" I shuddered as he traced one of his long fingernails across my throat as if teasing me.

"Marcus would have said anything to protect me.

He loved me, you see," he said, with something close to bile dripping from his fangs and onto my shirt. "My little brother thought he owed me for killing our mother. I was just six years old when I witnessed Marcus claw his way out of my mother's stomach. Seeing something like that just doesn't go away. It affects the mind – even the mind of a young vampire. It's haunted me my whole life, plagued my nightmares. I became obsessed by what I'd seen, I wanted to try and understand it in some way. So I took women off the streets and opened them, removed their uteruses, their intestines, just like my brother had done to our mother. When Marcus came back tonight and heard you closing the trap around me, he couldn't let me take the blame. Marcus felt guilty, you see, he felt responsible for creating the monster which he believed I had become. That's why Marcus was crying at my feet, begging for forgiveness. He wanted me to forgive him for what he had done, for turning me into a monster. But like I said, I don't do forgiveness. So I took off his head."

I knew that Drake was going to do to me what he had done to all those other women, but he was too strong to fight off. I glanced left, as he lowered his dripping mouth over my neck. I could see a flash of brown fur go rushing past the entrance to the mine, followed by the head of a vampire. It was then that I saw it, Drake's silver sword, lying just inches away. I splayed open my fingers as far as I could and felt for the sword. My fingertips brushed it. With Drake's teeth nipping my neck, I closed my eyes and made a desperate lunge for the sword. My fingers wrapped around it and I cried out as the edge of it sliced into my fingers. I could feel rivers of hot, sticky blood spilling onto my hands. Drake must have smelt it, as he brought his head up. In that moment, I gritted my teeth against the pain beating in my fingers like a heartbeat, and lifted up the sword. In one quick movement, I sliced it across Drake's back. With his eyes burning like cauldrons of fire in his face, he arched his back and screeched in pain.

I made a fist with my free hand and slammed it into his face. Drake's head snapped backwards and I seized my chance of rolling out from beneath him. I pulled myself to my feet and staggered towards the mouth of the mine. My legs wobbled beneath me as my heart raced in my ears. Drake screamed from behind me as he clawed his way along the rocky mine walls. I glanced back over my shoulder and could see his seething red eyes and white face racing towards me.

I looked front again, and screamed. Standing at the entrance to the mine were three – no four – werewolves.

"Oh, my God, Louise," I gasped, knowing that she was the fourth werewolf I could now see. With Drake fast approaching from behind, the werewolves made their way into the mine towards me. With my mind racing and heart slamming, I remembered Harry telling me that they could be killed by being pierced through the heart with a silver sword. I knew that Drake carried one, hidden within his walking stick, for that reason. So, brandishing it before me, I approached the werewolves.

"Don't make me kill you," I said to the preacher, who led his pack towards me, his white fur gleaming in the moonlight, which poured into the mine from behind them.

Seeing the sword, the preacher hesitated and took a step backwards. Sensing his fear of it, I moved forward, Drake's footsteps ringing in my ears. "I don't want to kill you, Preacher," I breathed. Then looking into the eyes of the wolf looming behind him, I knew it was Harry.

"Please, Harry, just let me out of here," I whispered, hoping that somewhere deep within him, he would understand and not hurt me. He howled angrily, and I waved the sword at them again. I looked at Zoe. Blood was swinging from her snout. Louise stood behind her, long thick black hair covering her body. Her eyes gleamed like two yellow moons on either side of her snout. "Louise," I whispered, "what did Zoe do to you?"

Louise made a growling noise in the back of her throat and snapped her giant jaws together. Drake was almost upon me now, so I lunged forward with the sword and the werewolves backed out and away from the front of the mine. Knowing that I had no way out or nowhere to go, I took the cigarette from behind my ear and lit it with my last remaining match. I could either go towards the Skinturners and become one of them, or head towards Drake and let him take me. Neither was an option I wanted.

"Thank you, Preacher," I shouted to the wolf and blew out the match.

The werewolves dropped to all fours and paced to and fro outside the entrance of the mine, like bored tigers caged in a zoo. They were waiting for me. The ground was covered with the bodies of the vampires that the werewolves had slain. I looked back over my shoulder as Drake approached, his mouth open wide. I pointed the sword at him.

"You can't kill me with that," he sneered.

"You're right," I said, bending down and snatching up one of the bundles of dynamite that I had placed by the mine entrance. "But I can kill you with this", I smiled, holding the fuse just beneath the cigarette that burned in the corner of my mouth.

"You wouldn't," Drake laughed.

Then looking back over my shoulder, I stared back at the werewolves. "Hey, Preacher," I shouted. "You said that maybe I had come back to stop whoever was killing those women back home. Well I think you were right. I can't think of any other reason why I would be here. I've either gone mad, or I really have gone back in time. But whatever the reason, I just want to go home."

The preacher leapt onto his back legs, and throwing

back his head, he howled up at the moon. I didn't know if he was trying to tell me that he understood. I guess I would never know. Then looking at Harry, I stared into his eyes, and said, "Thanks, Harry, I had fun!"

Turning to face Drake, I smiled, and with the burning end of the cigarette, I touched it to the fuse of the dynamite. There was a short flash of bright white light, searing heat, a deep booming sound like the loudest thunderclap and . . .

37

. . . and I sat up. The tube train rattled to a stop in Liverpool Street Underground Station. I looked about me as I used one of the handrails to pull myself up. The carriage was deserted. I spun around, and there was no one behind me. My heart was beating in my chest. I looked down at myself and I seemed to be intact, dressed in the same clothes that I had been wearing the night I had . . . I had what? Gone back to 1888? I was no longer wearing the rough woven denims, boots, long dark coat, hat, or gun belt. I was wearing my trainers, jeans, and jacket.

Feeling as if I had just gotten off a fairground ride, dizzy and faint, I staggered off the train and onto the deserted platform. "Hello?" I called out.

The only response I got was the beeping sound as

the train doors closed shut behind me. I watched the train pull out of the station and disappear into the tunnel. I looked at my watch and it read 23:56 hours, on the 9th of November 2012. I was back; but had I really gone?

I left the station and crossed the upper concourse and made my way out into the night. It was cold and raining, so I pulled up the collar of my coat and ran home.

I pushed open the door of my flat and was greeted by the orgasmic shrieks of delight coming from Sally's room. I passed down the landing to my room and closed the door. Everything seemed to look exactly as I had left it. My laptop was switched on as it always was, and next to it sat an overflowing ashtray and a pack of cigarettes. I took one and lit it. The smoke wasn't as thick as the cigarettes which the preacher had given me. But had there really been a preacher?

Beside the laptop was a half-full can of Coke. Coke! It was like finding gold. I snatched it up and took a mouthful. It was still fizzy as if I'd only opened it an hour or so ago. Hanging my sodden jacket on the back of my door, I sat before my laptop and checked the BBC News website. I searched it for stories of the recent murders in London. I couldn't find any articles that related to it. I typed in the words "Jack the Ripper copycat murders" into the news search engine and it came back with nothing. I then went to all the websites of all the national papers and searched them for any stories relating to Jack the Ripper-style killings that had happened in London over the last four months. Again, there was nothing.

I crushed out my cigarette in the ashtray, and with the sound of Sally moaning and groaning from the room next door, I typed in the names Spencer Drake and Marcus Dable into the search engine. Jumping back so violently from my seat that I knocked over the can of Coke, I stared at their names on the screen. With my hand shaking, I dragged the cursor over their names and clicked. There was a very small article about a Detective Sergeant Spencer Drake, and Police Surgeon Marcus Dable. The article stated that both had worked for Scotland Yard and had been part of the investigation team into the Jack the Ripper killings. At the request of Detective Inspector Frederick Abberline, both Spencer Drake and Marcus Dable had been sent to the United States of America in the later part of 1888 to follow up an enquiry into the Jack the Ripper killings. The report then went on to state that neither man were seen or heard of again, both believed to have died in a fatal mining accident, which had occurred as a result of an explosion while undertaking their enquiry. I scrolled down to the end of the article, and then clapped my hands over my mouth. Staring back at me from the screen were two faint and yellowed photographs of Drake and his younger brother.

With my hands shaking over the keyboard, I typed in the name "Harry Turner 1888." Nothing. I tried again, but this time I typed in "Harrison Turner 1888 Colorado." Nothing. I didn't know the preacher's real name, but I tried Zoe Edgar and Louise Pearson; still there was nothing about what had happened to my friends.

Had they really existed? I wondered, as I flopped onto my bed and pulled my jeans down over my hips. Had I really been back to 1888 and stopped a serial killer who would have gone on to commit murders one-hundred-and-twenty-four years later in London? Had I killed Jack the Ripper? Had it really been a vampire who had stalked those dark, narrow streets of Whitechapel over a hundred years ago, seeking out his prey? Is that why the murders stopped so suddenly back in 1888, because he died with me in some remote mine on the other side of the world?

But I didn't die, I thought. I was right here, trying to squeeze out of my rain-soaked jeans. It was then I felt something in my pocket. I reached inside, and gasping out loud, I pulled out the rosary beads I had taken from the chapel in the town of Black Water Gap. I jumped from my bed and went to my coat, which was hanging from the back of the door. I rummaged through the pockets in search of the crucifix, bottle of

holy water, and cloves of garlic I had when I was . . .
taken? They had gone.

Marley took them, I heard Zoe whisper in my ear.

I heard Sally cry out with joy from the room next
door and I thought of Louise. Holding my hands over
my ears, I threw myself onto my bed.

Six weeks passed, but it was like my life had stopped.
It hadn't moved on – or it was like I hadn't. What I
had seen, everything that I had done back in 1888,
seemed to fade that little bit more every time I opened
my eyes on a new day. I didn't want to lose those
memories of what had happened to me. I didn't want
to forget about the preacher, Zoe, Louise . . . *Harry*.
Every morning, as I lay on my bed reluctant to open
my eyes on a new day, knowing that my friends would
fade a little bit more, it was like I could hear Harry
whispering in my ear, *keep your eyes closed – if you
look at me, then this isn't real – it's just a fantasy.*

As I lay awake at night, listening to Sally whoop it up
with another new boyfriend, I tried to think of Harry and
remember what had happened between us, but even that
memory was fading. And however hard I tried to get those
feelings back on my own – it just wasn't the same.

Why had I been so keen to return? I would lay and
wonder. I had been a part of something back in 1888.
There had been adventure in my life – and some passion!
What did I have here? Not a great deal.

So of a night, when I couldn't sleep, I would go back to Aldgate Tube Station and ride the Circle Line, going around and around in those tunnels, searching the faces of fellow passengers, hoping that I would recognise something – recognise the man who had grabbed me around the throat. Maybe he could take me back again. But it was impossible – I hadn't seen his face. He could've been anyone. And when I got tired of going around and around in circles, I would watch the trains pass through the station. I would study the faces of each passenger.

Then one night, as I sat on a platform bench waiting for trains, I saw him get off and head up the platform towards the exit. It looked like him from the back, the same colour hair in the same scruffy style. He even had that arrogant slant to his walk. I rushed through the crowds, desperate not to lose sight of him before he disappeared amongst the throng of passengers heading for the exit. Reaching out, I grabbed his shoulder.

"Harry!" I said.

He turned and looked at me with a quizzical look.

"Sorry," I said, realising it wasn't him. "I thought you were someone else."

The man turned his back and headed for the exit. Tired and pissed off, I decided to go home and spend another lonely night wondering if I was going mad. Then I heard a song start up that I hadn't heard for years. My dad used to play it in the car when we went on